K

By Judi Jones

First print edition May 2016
KELLY PUBLICATIONS
01278 66 22 33
lynda@kellybooks.co.uk

Also published as an eBook
(ASIN B01EJUFJQ6) April 2016

ISBN: 13-digit: 978-1-903053-28-7
ISBN: 10-digit: 1-903053-28-5

Dedication:

To Mum – for encouraging me to dream
And Dad – for keeping my feet on the ground

Thank you for believing in me

K

My beautiful nightmare

Sometimes, when he walks towards me
Eyes flashing
I wonder
Does he want to kill me or kiss me?
I'm not entirely sure...
He's tormented by feelings of pain and confusion
He's tormented more by love
I know this because I feel it too
So, which does he want to do more
Kill me or Kiss me?
I'm not sure I mind either way...

Prologue

I will begin with how I know. How I know what she feels.
It's important that someone believes me.
It will help me hold on to my sanity.

They call this place a hospital. They say they're trying to make me better. What they're trying to do is make me normal, make me stop saying things they don't want to hear and most of all make me forget him.

I can't.

They think they're winning, which is why they're paying me special attention at the moment. I almost believed I was going insane, or as they like to put it "suffering from mental health issues". I began to think I had imagined him. That's why they removed anything that could do me serious damage, but I pulled a lot of my hair out, and my wrists still hurt from scratching them raw.

Now, I've realised something, which gives me hope. My favourite nurse, Lisa, has stopped feeling pity and started feeling afraid.

Why has she changed?
Why, unless she fears there is truth in what I say?
I know how she feels because I feel it too.

Even as a child, I knew I was different, but I didn't know why. I felt pain but had no idea where it came from, guilt without knowing what I'd done wrong and rage with no one to rage at.

My parents were not to blame. I was not abused as a child, and I was not neglected. I say this because my doctor seems to think I must have been, and my therapist – polite term for shrink – wants to know more about my parents than about me.

I don't hurt myself because I was hurt. I hurt myself because I know then that what I feel is real. It's the only way to be sure.

I remember the stomach pains; countless trips to the doctor for tests that came back negative.

"Stress perhaps," the doctor said.

At ten years old?

"What could she possibly be stressed about?" Mum asked.

I had no idea. I felt like a nuisance. I didn't realise it was other people's stress I was feeling, not then.

I remember friends coming to me upset, confused or angry. They would talk to me and leave calm, not happy, but more at peace. I would be left trying to shake off their feelings. They would take a piece of me and leave a piece of themselves. I didn't understand it, but as a teenager, I began to realise it was happening.

School was hard. I know I'm clever; my brain knows the answers, but trying to pinpoint the answer and write it down with so many emotions flooding my body was almost impossible. I constantly felt guilty, sad and ashamed, without ever knowing why.

Sometimes, I still become overwhelmed by emotions I don't understand, but I've learned to cope with it. Most of the time.

Throughout it all, books were my constant friends. Being able to escape was great, and somehow I felt I belonged more with the characters of a book than I did in real life. It gave me something to hold onto and helped me through the confusion.

My favourite book is Wuthering Heights with so many conflicting emotions tormenting the souls of poor Cathy and Heathcliff. It was as if Miss Bronte had taken every feeling known to man – or women – and stuffed them into one book. I felt like that. Like all those feelings had been amplified and stuffed into me. I ached with it.

I still love that book. I especially love the fact that I share a name with the Author. Emily, that is.

I am Emily Naish. Twenty-one last month and still daydreaming.

K1

One year ago…

I stood looking up at the old Georgian Manor with hope fluttering inside of me. I knew it was only a cleaning job, but it was a new start and the house promised peace and hard work, both of which I needed.

As I walked up the steps, the door opened. Surprised, I stopped. Had someone been looking out for me? A man with sandy coloured hair, no older than thirty, stepped through the door and smiled. "Hello. I'm Lord Ashton. Very pleased to meet you."

"Oh… Hello." I stuttered, surprised to be greeted by the Lord of the manor rather than a butler. Seeing the kindness in his face, I relaxed and smiled back. I felt it before he shook my hand; his feelings – a mixture of sadness and despair – were easy to pick up.

He showed me into a room with high ceilings, fluted coving and antique furniture. In the centre of the room stood an oval table, a newspaper was left open at one end. He ushered me to a pair of carved easy chairs by the window. I settled myself into one, and he sat in the other.

The interview didn't go well to begin with.

"Do you have any references?"

"Well, yes, as a childminder."

"I don't need a childminder." He answered, frowning.

"Umm… No, but it takes a lot of cleaning, looking after children. What with all the craft… and nappies." Why was I talking about nappies? I felt my cheeks redden.

I have no idea how I thought I would get the job. I hoped not too many had applied. I looked down at my dress; it seemed pretty when I put it on, but now it looked silly. Why didn't I wear something more business like? Even if I hadn't been able to sense what Lord Ashton felt, I could see it in his face. I needed to do something.

I held his eyes, determined to hook him into giving me a chance. "May I be honest?"

"Have you been lying up until now, Miss Naish?" His eyebrows twitched upwards.

I laughed, relaxing my shoulders. "No, but I've been trying to say what I think you want to hear. May I tell you a bit about myself?"

He nodded, "Please, go ahead."

"My husband left me a month ago, and I can't afford to keep paying the mortgage on the house, so I'm selling it. I'm moving in with a friend temporarily. I was working as a child-minder from my home, so I can't continue with that job."

His eyes narrowed. "So any job will do?"

I swallowed and pushed on. "In a way, yes, but there's a special reason why I want this job."

He raised his eyebrows, so I continued.

"When I was child, I was a dreamer. My Dad used to say I was away with the fairies half the time." I looked up and met his eyes. "You see, lots of my dreams were about this house. I can't believe I'm actually here. When I saw the advert, well... you can imagine, I had to apply. Working here would be amazing."

He tilted his head. "How did you know this house; you can't even see it from the road?"

I looked out of the window. "If you could take me to one of the rooms at the east end, I'll show you."

The feelings I'd felt coming so strongly from him had slunk quietly into the background. He seemed amused and curious. He stood up, signalling that I could continue my tale.

"May we go to the room the other side of the– do you call it a hall?"

"It would have been called the grand hall, but I think hall will do. Why do you need to go into the drawing room?"

"I want to show you something out of the window."

He led the way from the room, which I guessed he used as a breakfast room, into the drawing room, a dim room despite the morning sun. Rich reds and oak made it seem luxurious rather than depressing.

I walked to the window and looked down through the trees to the edge of town. I searched until I found the house where I grew up. "When I was a child, I used to look out of our bathroom window to the hills in the distance. I spent hours gazing at a beautiful house on the hillside. It was half hidden by the trees, but I could tell it was old and grand. In the winter, if I borrowed Dad's binoculars, I could really see it – the chimneys, the windows, and the grand pillars either side of the door. I loved the way it peered mysteriously between the evergreens. I imagined the wealthy people who must live there." I twisted around to see Lord Ashton studying me. "Yes," I confirmed. "I'm talking about this house; Kenwood Manor."

He smiled.

I returned my gaze to the edge of town and pointed. "There. That was my house. You can see part of the roof and the white wall at the end."

After a pause, he said, "Ah, yes, I see it."

I faced him and waited until his eyes turned to mine. "I used to dream I would live here one day. I know that's impossible, but I would be honoured to help look after it."

He smiled, and I could feel it. He radiated warmth and pleasure.

"Can you start tomorrow?"

I smiled a real smile too.

Having agreed to arrive at nine am the next day, Lord Ashton showed me to the front door. He paused, his hand on the door knob. "I need you to promise me something."

Anxiety skittered around in my chest. *Don't be stupid, why be worried? He looks harmless enough. Or is that his feeling I'm getting? Even more stupid. Why would he be anxious?* With no idea what to say, I nodded and waited.

"I want you away before dark each day. I don't like to think of you travelling home in the dark."

Surprised, I blurted, "It's not far."

The anxiety hadn't abated and his face looked serious. "Even so, I take the safety of my employees seriously."

"I understand..." that you're a bit of a fusspot, but nice, so, "I promise I'll be away before dark."

His face relaxed into a smile and the anxiety retreated. He opened the door and it took all my restraint not to skip down the steps. My battered car was soon crunching along the gravel drive. Half way along, I glanced at the rear-view mirror. Lord Ashton was still there, watching me drive away.

The following day, I arrived punctually to start my new job at Kenwood Manor. Lord Ashton briefly welcomed me, gave me a list of chores to do, showed me where to find everything I needed, then left me to it. I kept my head down and worked hard.

Having tidied and cleaned the kitchen, I looked at my watch – 4:15...I have to be away by 4:30... it won't take long to take this bread out for the birds. Grabbing the crusts, I slipped out of the back door to find somewhere to leave them.

Soon, I was daydreaming as I kicked the multi-coloured leaves across the grass, wondering if the Manor grounds would be as beautiful in the summer as they were on that autumnal day. I felt excited at the thought of seeing the changes through the seasons. The light was fading and I turned to head back to the house, but then I noticed a partially boarded window.

I went straight over and pressed my nose to the glass, trying to peer through. Inside was completely dark.

"Miss Naish, I presume?"

I swung around and, with a shriek, I managed to fall over. So, the very first time I saw Karl, I was lying on my back splattered in mud.

How had this strange man got so close without me sensing him?

He smirked, towering over me in the half-light. I had no idea who he was.

"Shush! I won't hurt you."

He offered his hand, but I ignored it and scrambled to my feet. What right did he have to creep up on me? "Who are you?" I demanded, with more confidence than I felt.

Even standing, I had to crane my neck to look up at him. I felt myself blush as his startling green eyes danced over me. He was somehow familiar, though I was sure I'd never met him. I would have remembered if I had. He ran his hand through his jet-black hair; I found myself putting my hand over my racing heart.

I felt no emotion from him, nothing at all. This had never happened, not at this close range. He was almost close enough to touch, but he might as well have been miles away. It was disconcerting to say the least, and I was tempted to reach out and touch him to see if he was real.

"I'm Karl Ashton; I'm a distant relation of Tom. I'm staying here."

"He hasn't mentioned you." I frowned. My head was telling me to run, but he had a magnetism that held me to the spot. Then I remembered my promise to Lord Ashton, that I would finish work and be away before dark. What with being nosy and daydreaming, I hadn't noticed the sun disappearing.

"I need to go; I should have left already." I mentally pulled away from him, then started to edge around him physically, but he blocked my way, saying, "Wait!" with a voice so full of authority that I froze to the spot. A tingle ran up and down my spine.

He spoke quickly. "He wouldn't have mentioned me, and you shouldn't tell him you've seen me."

"Why on earth not?"

He studied my face, then said, "Because I gave my word I'd stay away from you."

I hesitated, staring at him. "Why would he say that?"

He just stared back at me with those green eyes.

I folded my arms. "I should certainly tell him. Please let me pass."

As soon as he stepped aside, I felt disappointed; I had no excuse to linger.

"Emily!" This was Lord Ashton now, wondering where I was no doubt.

"I'm coming," I called back. I glanced at the stranger and hurried towards the east corner of the Manor house. He fell quickly into step beside me; I felt flustered.

"If you tell Tom, he will find an excuse to stop you coming here." His mouth was close to my ear. I shuddered as his cool breath tickled my skin.

"But, why?" I said, trying to ignore the wonderful sensations in my body.

"Let's just say I have a bad track record with women."

I gulped. *For God's sake, woman, get a grip! So what if he's hot. He's obviously trouble.* I did my best to look casual. "He doesn't need to worry about me. I'm not taken in by good looks." *Damn. Why did I say that?*

Through the dusk, I recognised Lord Ashton marching around the corner of the walled garden and felt his anxiety seconds later. I glanced sideways, but the stranger had gone.

Running up to my boss, I launched into a garbled explanation. "I'm so sorry! I know you don't like me being out here in the dark, but I took some stale bread out for the birds and completely lost track of time." I spoke quickly, hoping to reassure him. I knew he was a fuss pot, but he was kind and I liked him.

He looked at the muddy state of my clothes and frowned.

"Oh, I slipped. I'm not hurt, though. Don't worry."

He smiled, and I felt him relax. I asked him if he would mind fetching my coat as I didn't want to go inside covered in mud, but he insisted I went in. I stood, wondering about Karl.

There I was, feeling dirty and out of place in the grand, yes grand, hallway. Why hadn't I told Lord Ashton about my encounter with Karl?

As I waited for my coat, I admired the sweeping staircase and the family portraits on the wall going up. My eyes rested on one in particular, the one nearest to me at the bottom. It was of a tall man wearing a powdered wig of the age. The face was the same, and those green eyes were the same as the ones I saw moments ago. At least it proved the stranger in the garden was family. I went forward and read the plaque at the bottom of the frame: Lord Karl Ashton 1760 – 1796.

I stepped back from the painting and shuddered.

K2

November…

It was a glorious sunny day as I headed towards the woods in the manor grounds. I was taking my morning break and the crisp air was a pleasant change from the dust I was constantly battling. The grass was still white with frost in places, and I pulled my cardigan tighter. The Rhododendrons gave way to evergreens and the path became a track. I couldn't resist continuing into the trees. I've always loved woods and the forest; there's so much hidden nature there and paths to explore.

When I came to a small round clearing, my eyes immediately fell on a small marble grave stone. Intrigued, I picked my way over moss and earth to reach it. I thought perhaps the grave belonged to a family dog and crouched to read the inscription. What I read filled me with sadness: Tobias Ashton – Beloved Son – 1804-1808. I wondered whose son Tobias had been, and why he had died so young. I felt he must be lonely in that tiny grave in the woods, and I worried that he had been forgotten. Looking around me, I spotted some flowering Ivy. I carefully broke some away from the trees and laid it gently on the small mound of the grave. "Goodbye, Tobias", I whispered, "I'll come and visit you again soon, I promise."

As I returned to the house, I met Lord Ashton, his boots crunching across the gravel path.

"I'm just going to see to the horses," he informed me, with a warm smile.

He went across to the stables every afternoon at the same time to fetch in his two mares. He talked about them a lot and obviously enjoyed caring for them himself. "They love going out in the morning, and they look forward to coming in again for their corn and a good grooming. Looking after animals is good for the soul."

I smiled and nodded, hoping I would have a pet of my own one day. "Okay, I'll have tea and biscuits ready when you come back, as usual." I headed for the house, still amazed that I could just walk into the home of my childhood dreams.

In the kitchen, I filled the kettle, set out a tray, and then watered the plants along the windowsill. The autumn sun was beginning to sink in the sky, which meant I would soon have to leave. I'd reminded Lord Ashton that I'm an adult and drive home in a car, but he was adamant and promised it would not affect my pay. So, with the autumn nights drawing in, I had to leave work earlier and earlier.

I wiped down the worktops and cleaned the sink. There were other things I didn't understand. He had explained that some doors were locked because the rooms weren't fit for use. Also, he insisted that I was only to use the main stairs as the others were unsafe. This was a nuisance because it would have been easier to use the back stairway at times, with it being nearer the kitchen. I didn't complain though; the hours suited me just fine. Getting home early gave me plenty of time to meet friends, or visit my family.

As well as cleaning, I had started cooking lunch, and Lord Ashton insisted I ate with him. I knew he liked the company.

"My last cleaner, Mrs Jennings, would never have agreed to join me for lunch," he told me, waving his fork in the air. "Most improper, she would say in her stern matronly voice. I didn't dare argue with her. She was good to me, though. She worked here for thirty years."

"Why did she leave?" I asked.

"She was seventy-two last month. She kept going as long as she could, but it was getting too much."

"I'm not surprised!" I laughed.

It was more like having lunch with a friend than an employer. I talked about my friends and my family; he talked about business ventures and about the house and his horses. He never mentioned family, not once.

There was certainly plenty to occupy my mind as I went about my chores. I fantasised about the families that had lived in the manor, and the four-year-old boy in the grave. Had his short life been happy? One way or another, my thoughts always returned to the mysterious stranger, Karl. Where exactly was he sleeping? Why was he never around for lunch? Was it just coincidence that he bore such a canny resemblance to the Karl in the portrait? I found myself longing to see him and imagining scenarios in which we would meet. Each of these fantasies left my heart beating faster.

The following day, having cleaned the kitchen floor, I carried the dirty water through the old scullery, heading for the outside drain. On my way through the rear hall, I noticed the open doorway, one that was normally locked. I was sure it had been the window of this room I was trying to peer into the week before when I was surprised by Karl.

I stood looking at the door for what seemed like ages. I couldn't have opened it, and I couldn't imagine Lord Ashton leaving it open, not after all his warnings. That left one other option. I swallowed hard and tried to slow my breathing.

I drifted towards the doorway and looked inside. The room was lit by lamps as there was so little natural light coming in through the boarded window.

I sensed something, looked to the side and gasped; he stood a few feet away, his eyes fixed on me. I felt my face turn scarlet and noticed the hint of muscles beneath his dark red shirt. Even dressed casually in dark jeans, he looked smart. I suddenly felt shabby in my apron.

"Good afternoon." His face gave away nothing.

What should I do? Run probably, but if he intended to harm me, there was not much I could do to stop him.

"Hello," I mumbled.

"Do come in; I want to talk to you."

I stayed in the doorway, half afraid, half excited. For a moment, fear won. I turned to walk away. "I need to finish my work."

"I'm sure you're allowed a break. And we both know his Lordship won't be back for at least an hour."

I turned back to him, suspicion crawling through my mind. I could hear my dad saying I'd read too many fairy tales, but I couldn't shake what I sensed. I took a deep breath, then spoke, my legs trembling. "Okay, I usually take my break in the conservatory." I paused, then blurted, "I love the sunlight. Don't you?"

In the silence, my heart beat faster, wondering why I was asking him about sunlight and wondering what he would say.

Finally, he spoke, his tone even. "I would rather stay here. I have a headache, and the bright light will make it worse."

I stared at him, transfixed. Even in the dim light of the room, I could see the piercing green of his eyes. My mind filled with an image of the portrait. Those same eyes in a man who lived long ago, and died young. The words tumbled out: "You look better without the wig."

He blinked rapidly, then looked down at his hands. "I meant what I said before; I won't hurt you."

I gasped. He hadn't denied it. *But...that means... Why aren't I running? Stay calm, Emily.* "Why should I believe you?" I took a step backwards, but his eyes burned into mine. Those beautiful green eyes. "Because you promised Lord Ashton?"

"No, because I'm very bored and I find you Interesting." He stepped towards me, his eyes holding me rooted to the spot.

"You're making fun of me." I felt small and foolish beneath his gaze.

He chuckled, "Admittedly, I do find you amusing. Are you aware you talk to the house as you clean it?"

Determined not to make a complete fool of myself, I pulled back my shoulders and rested my hands on my hips to stop them shaking. "I'm glad you find it funny." I didn't; I was fuming. "What happens when you're bored of me too? Will you harm me then? Only, if you're going to kill me, I'd rather you just got on with it."

"No, Emily." My name fell softly from his lips, leaving me weak like a kitten. I would like someone I can talk too. Ned's okay, but dull as ditch water. As for the last cleaner. I thought she'd never leave, miserable old bat. I only tolerated the woman because she was good at her job, and kept her mouth shut about me. You're different. You're young and full of energy. And you seem honest. I think I can trust you."

"Actually, if I were trustworthy, I would have told Lord Ashton about meeting you."

"Ah, but you see, technically I am Lord Ashton. I have only let him assume the title because I am presumed dead and gone. As far as I can see, you've been loyal to me and to the house. Nothing else matters."

"So, I was right then, you are a…." I couldn't quite bring myself to say it out loud.

"A vampire. Yes, I am a vampire, and yes, that is my portrait. That wig looks ridiculous, doesn't it?"

Despite myself, I laughed. How on earth I could find anything funny about the situation, I don't know, and yet I wasn't as surprised as I should have been. Hadn't I always known there was more to the world than the obvious? I guess my laugh was partly due to nerves; it felt strange to be alone with a man, where the only feelings I could feel were my own.

I confess, my feelings were both confusing and increasingly overwhelming. In truth, I was more excited than afraid, my eyes still fixed on his, unable to look away.

"You don't look that afraid of me." He smiled in a way that, for once, looked sincere. I wished I could tell.

"I'm afraid of lots of things, but death isn't one of them," I answered honestly.

"So what are you afraid of?"

"You must take me for an idiot if you think I would tell you that." I was lost, not being able to read him.

"Maybe when you know me better?"

I doubted it and said, "I should go now."

"Do you know where you'll be cleaning tomorrow afternoon?" He took a step towards me. I was startled and flattered by his interested. My stomach twisted and my pulse quickened.

"Lord Ashton said something about me cleaning the library. Do you mind me referring to him as Lord?"

"That's fine, I suppose, but please call me Karl."

The name ran through my head: I loved it. Karl. Suddenly fearful he might be making a fool of me, I scrambled for words, any words. "Lord Ashton wants me to start dusting the books." I could have kicked myself. Was that really the best thing I could say to him?

"Draw the library curtains when he goes to do the horses. I can keep you company and talk to you while you work." His eyes danced over me.

Blushing furiously, I turned away and grabbed my mop and bucket. My brain was screaming NO! My heart was crashing hard against my chest. What on earth was I getting into?

When I looked back, the door was closed.

The next day, I was anxious all morning and kept dropping things. Despite what Karl said, I did feel disloyal to Lord

Ashton – junior. Lunch was a disaster. I scalded myself trying to hard-boil eggs, and dropped the mayonnaise jar, causing glass and goo to go everywhere. Lord Ashton came rushing in and helped me clear up, which left me embarrassed, hot, and not a bit hungry.

"You don't seem yourself today. Would you like the afternoon off?"

I should have said yes, but instead, I mumbled something about being a bit hormonal, to which he smiled politely, went bright red, and sidled out of the room.

At least it was cool in the library. I was thankful to be dusting books and not the best Wedgewood. The house faced south-east and the library was situated on the north corner. This helped to keep the books protected from the sunlight. Normally I would have hated being in a cool, dull room, but with thoughts of Karl heating my blood, I was glad.

Damn him. I'd let him get me into this state, and I was cross with myself. I wondered if I should ignore him and leave the curtains open. He was certainly arrogant enough to assume I would do as he said. Perhaps this was a good reason not to. But what if he turned up anyway?

I busied myself with dusting books, and managed to avoid the curtains for another twenty minutes before I pulled the heavy velvet across and shut the autumn light out.

I half expected him to burst in straight away, but he didn't, so I carried on with the books, looking at the spines as I went. I recognised a few of the authors, like Wordsworth, Keats and Blake, and it annoyed me that they didn't seem to be in any sensible order. I was muttering about it under my breath when I heard a laugh.

I spun round to see him settled in a leather armchair behind me, eyebrows raised and a smug look on his face. Damn him, I thought. I hadn't felt him there. I wasn't used to being near people without feeling anything.

"So, you talk to the books as well."

"I find them good company; they don't mock me or treat me like a fool."

He rested his long fingers on the arm of the chair and leaned forward. "Oh come on; I only mock you because you seem perfectly able to defend yourself. It's more fun than polite conversation, don't you think?"

I was struck again by his green eyes. They seemed to pin me to the spot. I felt hot and uncomfortable, and wanted to shift the focus away from myself. "Can I ask you a question?"

"You may, and I may even answer."

"Obviously, it's true about vampires and sunlight, so are the other myths about them true, like garlic and mirrors?"

"No, complete nonsense and the sunlight bit is only partly true. We are very sensitive to it and prefer not to go out in daylight. Our skin would burn quickly and it hurts our eyes, but we don't instantly combust like they show in films."

"What about flying? Can you fly?"

"I've answered one question already; now you must answer mine. It was me who wanted to talk to you, remember?"

I twisted the duster between my fingers. "Okay, what did you want to know?"

He shifted in his chair and fixed his eyes on mine. "My question is," he said with an even tone, "why did you put flowers on the grave?"

I was taken aback, and couldn't read his feelings. Had I done something wrong? "You mean the child's grave in the woods?"

His eyes held mine. "Yes."

"Lord Ashton said it was okay for me to walk around the grounds in my break." *Why is he questioning me? He's not my boss.* I lifted my chin and crossed my arms. Ned has already told me off for going in the woods, so I'm sorry if I did wrong, but I didn't know it would be a problem."

"I didn't say there was a problem, but you haven't answered me. Why the flowers for someone you never knew?"

I shrugged. "It was the natural thing to do. I couldn't leave it unattended like that. No child deserves to be forgotten."

His eyes pierced into mine with an intensity I'd never seen before. "He has not been forgotten!"

For a moment, I felt something from him, but then it was gone. "I'm sorry."

"Don't apologise," he said. "Actually, I'd welcome you doing it every week."

Bewildered, I nodded weakly. "I intended to, but who is he? Who is the child in the grave?"

"And take no notice of Ned." He continued as if I hadn't asked a question. But he shifted his gaze away from mine. "He probably thinks I go on the rampage out there in the shadows."

My heartbeat quickened, and the grave fell from my mind. I was suddenly aware of being alone with him, and even though I was standing and he was sitting, I felt small. "So... do you go on the rampage?" I looked down at the duster I was twisting in my hands, afraid of what I would hear.

His gaze met mine. "Not anymore. There was a time when no one would have been safe from me, but that was a long-time ago."

I swallowed hard. "And now? Am I safe?"

"Yes, of course!" His eyes were wide, imploring. He suddenly moved to get up and I shifted backwards. I pulled in a sharp breath and pressed my back to the bookshelf. He stopped, holding his palms up. "I'm not going to hurt you, Emily." He sunk back into the chair.

Letting out my breath, I tried to calm my trembling body. Part of me wanted to run, but I was caught like a moth near a flame. I was aware of the blood pulsing through my body. My hand moved to my neck. "Do you…need blood?"

He looked at his hands and nodded. "Yes, but I don't need to kill for it, not now. Even chaos can become tedious after a while. I wanted logic and order, and to be in control of myself again. Another vampire, we call him Prof, figured out a way to synthesize human blood. You have no reason to be afraid." He stood up and stepped towards me.

I was frozen to the spot. I desperately wanted to believe him. "I'm not sure I trust you?"

"I don't blame you if you don't, but I have no reason to lie to you. Besides, I trust you. Believe me, as far as females are concerned, that's a first."

He moved away and perched on the edge of another armchair.

I relaxed my muscles and scrambled my wits together. "I'm the first woman you've ever trusted? But you don't know anything about me!" His green eyes looked sad. I took a step towards him. "Tell me why you don't want to be discovered, who could hurt you, and how?"

"If I tell you, you must tell me what you are afraid of."

I slid into the chair he'd vacated. "Okay, but you first."

Karl slid his chair closer to mine and settled himself into its velvet luxury. He leant towards me and spoke softly. "UVA rays could kill a vampire, but it doesn't happen instantly; more like a slow burn. According to legend, there have been vampire hunters for as long as there have been vampires. I have met a few and killed them. They used to try trapping us in the open, but we are too fast and strong. They've tried different weapons, which have hurt us, but not destroyed us. At times, hunters have been successful by knocking buildings down over sleeping vampires and exposing them to the sun.

Personally, I've never been too concerned, but it would not do to become complacent."

He sat back and smiled. "Your turn."

I hesitated, then told him the truth. "I'm afraid of losing my identity… and my mind."

"That's cheating. What does it even mean?"

"It means I have so much going on inside my head most of the time, I'm never sure what's real. Meeting a vampire hasn't helped, but I've always been the same. Complicated, I suppose you would call me. Anyway, it isn't cheating because it's true."

The grandfather clock behind me chimed three.

I gasped. "Oh no! I'm meant to have a pot of tea ready in half an hour, and I've hardly touched these books."

"You dust them; I'll put them back." He smiled again and stood beside me. It was hard to believe I was standing close to a vampire. He was probably the most dangerous man I had ever met, but I no longer feared him. Not that I could relax, but I quite liked the feeling of nervous butterflies somersaulting in my stomach.

"Do you like reading?" he asked.

"Yes, when I have the time. I like to escape into fiction."

"You shouldn't be so keen to escape your life; immortality isn't all it's cracked up to be."

I looked at him, expecting him to be smiling, but he wasn't.

"What particular books do you like?" he asked.

It seemed strange talking about mundane things after our previous conversation, but I enjoyed him showing an interest.

"Different types. Wuthering Heights is my favourite."

"Heathcliff was a jerk, pining over a woman."

"Do you think so? I always thought Cathy was daft for letting him go."

"Then perhaps they were both stupid. If you want to read it again, we have it here somewhere. A first edition, I believe."

"It must be worth a fortune! I couldn't possibly borrow it." I stared at the books I was dusting, suddenly afraid of damaging them.

"Books are meant to be read, and Tom certainly doesn't bother with them, so you may as well."

I thanked him, but had no intention of taking him up on the offer. My mind wandered again to his earlier question and why he would want me to put flowers on the grave.

"The boy, in the grave – Tobias, isn't it?"

"Yes, but I call him Toby."

"Was he your son?"

"Yes, but that's a story for another time." He placed the last of the dusted books on the shelf and turned to leave. "Don't forget the curtains."

I nodded and glanced towards them. When I turned back, he was gone. But not all of him. I felt sure he had left behind the tiniest wisp of a feeling, coiling itself around my heart. It was hard to identify, but it seemed like hope.

Whilst drinking tea with Lord Ashton, I asked about the locked room on the first floor. He looked at me sharply, and I apologised for being nosy.

"It's okay. It's no big secret, but it's a rather sad story." He replaced his cup in the saucer. "Many years ago, in the eighteenth century, a young boy who lived here died in an accident with his mother. That room was his nursery. It was shut up and never entered again, to my knowledge. I keep it locked out of respect." He smiled and then got up, "Now let's talk about nicer things. I'm going out riding with a friend tomorrow and would like to offer him lunch when we return.

Would you mind going to the shops in the morning and buying something appropriate?"

"No, of course I don't mind. I'll make sure the dining room is warm."

"Splendid."

Driving home, I thought about Lord Ashton's words and the grave in the woods. Only one grave, but two people had died in the accident. I wondered what had happened to the mother.

K3

I didn't see Karl again for several days. I was on edge all the time, but managed to provide a decent enough lunch for Lord Ashton and his friend. I couldn't shake the feeling that Karl was staying away deliberately, to make me wonder where he was. I was getting more annoyed with him each day and even more annoyed with myself for caring. I told myself I was intrigued with the mystery, it wasn't as if I fancied him; I was just curious.

I'd tried distracting myself by finding out some more about the house from Lord Ashton. He often stopped to talk to me as I worked; on this occasion, he found me dusting pictures in the grand hall. Grand it was; dominated by a huge curved stairway, leading to a balcony landing. The hall was once used to host parties and still housed a grand piano.

Tom's ancestor, Lord Anthony Ashton, had the house built in 1758, soon after his marriage to Mary Kenwood, whom he named the house after. He also commissioned the building of several cottages for workers and a few shops to supply them. Gradually, the small town of Kenwood had evolved with a variety of houses.

Kenwood Manor had been traditionally decorated, and modern touches, like the central heating, were well hidden. There was little feminine input; no cushions in the chairs, no portraits of women, and the only ornaments were brass horses.

By the Wednesday, I thought Karl must have tired of me already, and I felt disappointed. That afternoon, after grooming the horses, Lord Ashton announced he would be away the next day on business. He told me I could have the day off on full pay, and to enjoy myself.

At first, I was glad at the chance of a day off. My best friend would be working, but I could visit my parents, or go into town. Then I thought of Karl, and a thrill ran through my body. Maybe he would visit me while Tom was away. *How on earth am I going to persuade Lord Ashton I want to work on my day off?* I had to try. "You don't need to pay me for a day off. I'd be happy to work in the garden with Ned if you don't want me in the house on my own."

His eyes narrowed and I sensed his anxiety. "Now you mustn't think I don't trust you, Miss Naish. I just think you deserve some time off for all your hard work."

I pressed on; I had to persuade him. "I get paid for the work I do, so you should expect me to work hard. I would rather make up the time, or I would feel bad about taking the money."

He frowned. "But why would you want to work when I will pay you to have a day to yourself?"

Looking at my hands, I decided to tell a part truth. "My personal life isn't exactly fun at the moment. My best friend, who I lodge with, will be working. If I'm on my own doing nothing… well, I'll just think about how my marriage fell apart. To be honest, you'll be doing me a favour if you let me come here. It makes me happy." I looked up at him, hoping my wide eyes would persuade him.

He smiled, but I noticed his furtive glances towards the house. "Well…alright, I'll speak to Ned. There's always plenty to do in the garden."

"Would you allow me to dig a small garden for vegetables somewhere tomorrow? If you agree, I could plant some things now, like carrots and purple sprouting broccoli, and next year I can plant salad and fruit bushes. Imagine having your lunch fresh from the garden and…"

"Okay, okay, stop! I agree" He held his hands up in surrender at my onslaught of enthusiasm. "Make sure you don't hurt your back digging, though. And make sure you leave before dark."

I grinned and nodded. "I will, I promise"

"Let me talk to Ned, I'll say it's my idea. I'll ask him to suggest a spot and help you dig it."

"Thanks, I'll enjoy it."

He gave me money for plants and told me to buy lunch in town as well. I put the money in my purse and saw a folded piece of paper I didn't recognise. It simply said:

> *Don't forget the flowers*
> ## K

He's got some nerve! It's nearly a week since I saw him and he's giving me commands. I'll do it for Toby, not for him. In truth, I was glad he had remembered me. I folded the note carefully and put it back in my purse.

I hadn't seen much of Ned and had found him quite grumpy, so I wasn't sure how he would respond to me poking around in the garden. He lived in the old gatehouse, and as far as I knew, never went into the manor house at all.

The grounds were extensive, but much of it was woodland and a self-employed tree surgeon was brought in to manage this. A few fields had been let to neighbouring farmers for their cattle to graze.

Ned used a big ride-on mower for the lawn, but even so, with all the flower beds and the pond, there was a lot of work. I had no idea how old he was. He looked weathered, but he seemed quite fit. I guessed he was about sixty.

The following morning, dressed in jeans, wellies, and a chunky sweater, I drove to Kenwood Manor as usual, but stopped outside the gatehouse. I spotted Ned trundling along his garden path with a wheelbarrow full of gardening tools. I pulled over and got out. "Good morning," I called and approached him cautiously.

He turned and nodded in my direction. "I've dug a patch down by the stream. That way you can water the plants easier in the summer. Do you know what you're doing?"

I felt myself blush, suddenly aware of how little I knew about gardening. I picked up a slight feeling of disdain from him, but nothing worse. I smiled warmly, hoping to win him over. "I wasn't expecting you to have dug it already, but thanks; it's really kind of you."

"Yes, well, I don't have time to hang about."

I sensed his embarrassment mixed with a tinge of pleasure, so I continued. "To be honest, I only know a little from planting things with some children I used to look after. I was hoping you would advise me. It's obvious you have green fingers; those fuchsias look amazing."

His face brightened slightly, but I sensed he was wary.
He looked towards the fuchsias, hand on hips. "It's been a mild autumn this year, so the flowers have lasted well. I dare say I could give you some advice."

"Thanks. I'd love to pick your brains," I said, glad to feel him relax. We chatted about vegetables that would grow over winter, and he suggested things I would need to improve the soil and look after them. By the time we had finished talking, he had told me some gardening tips that his father had told him. Waving good-bye, I noticed a twinkle in his eye.

I drove to town with Karl on my mind. *I need to get back from town as quickly as I can. That way he'll have more chance of seeing me. But how will I get inside the house?* The sun hung low in the sky and I squinted in its glare. I adjusted the sun visor. *He's hardly likely to come out into the garden in broad daylight.*

The road still glistened in patches where the frost lingered, and I drove cautiously along the main street. I was still worrying about seeing Karl when I noticed a flash of white in front of me. I slammed on the brakes.

I skidded to a halt inches away from a black and white springer spaniel, who was now standing on the pavement with a ball in its mouth. Gripping the wheel with trembling hands, I watched as a girl came running out of the park to retrieve her dog. *Thank God there was nothing behind me.* The girl waved at me sheepishly, then disappeared with the spaniel in tow.

I continued around the corner to the garden centre and, still shaken, headed straight for the coffee shop. Whilst sipping my cappuccino and nibbling a chocolate brownie, my mind wandered back to the manor, and Karl: *Where there's a will there's a way!* My mum's words sprang into my head. If I went around the back of the house, in the shade near one of the windows. Maybe, if he really wanted to see me...my heart sank again...who was I trying to kid?

My mood brightened as I pushed a trolley around the centre collecting all the things I needed. No matter what happened, I knew I would enjoy planting the vegetable garden and watching it grow. Not wanting to hang around in town any longer, I returned to the coffee shop and bought some sandwiches with the money Tom had given me.

Driving back, I tried hard to keep my mind on the road. I didn't want any more near misses. As I came to the big iron manor gates, I had a strange feeling I was returning home.

Once inside the big iron gates of Kenwood Manor, I began unloading my purchases into the wheelbarrow. I noticed Ned working in the flower beds near the house and, having exchanged a wave, I decided I'd better head straight for the patch of earth he'd dug. I was soon digging, planting and labelling, trying hard to convince myself not to go loitering behind the house, on the off chance Karl would appear. *Why am I being such a fool over him?*

At two o'clock, I rinsed my hands in the stream and ate my sandwiches. I noticed some Michaelmas Daisies growing beside the hedgerow and decided they would be perfect for my other errand.

As I crossed the lawn and headed for the woods, I noticed Ned going into his cottage. *Perhaps I could take a walk behind the house in a minute. I shook my head at my own stupidity and continued to the tiny grave.*

The sun was peering through the trees, and it lit up the gravestone. I crouched down and ran a finger over the name – TOBIAS. Karl had said he called him Toby. I tried to imagine him calling out to the young boy. Had he played with him? Had they walked here together? Did the little boy know he was loved? I hoped so.

As I placed the flowers on the soft grass, I wondered how Karl had coped with losing his son. And was it his wife who died too? I closed my eyes and tried to imagine the horror he must have felt.

When I opened my eyes and stood up, something shiny caught my eye. Just beside the grave was an arrow cut from aluminium foil and weighed down with a stone. I looked around and found another one. I felt a strange excitement fluttering in my stomach. It had to be Karl's work, surely. I followed the arrows until I came to a dark hole in the ground. It was square and had ladder rungs leading down from it. Nearby was what looked like a hatch covered with grass and moss. I knelt down and peered down the hole. A light came on somewhere below me.

"Come down!"

I recognised the voice at once, but pretended I didn't. My heart quickened its pace. "Who is that, and why would I want to climb down into a hole in the ground?"

"You know full well who it is," the voice called back. "I thought you'd be interested to see where I live."

"I thought you lived in those rooms at the back of the house." It seemed ridiculous yelling down a hole at him, but I was reluctant to go down.

"Don't be silly; you know I wouldn't consign myself to servants' quarters. I'm better than that."

"So why bother talking to a mere servant?" *Arrogant bastard!* "I'm sure you could find worthier company than me. Goodbye." I stepped away from the edge. His voice followed me.

"Wait! I don't think of you as a servant. You may be Tom's servant, but I would prefer it if you were my friend."

Does he mean friend or something more? I wish I could tell. I stepped back to the hole and crouched at the edge. "Why?"

His face came into view; his eyes peering up at me. "Because I've never had one. I wondered if it would make my existence more interesting."

Is he teasing me? "You've never had a friend! Not even before, when you were human?"

"No, never wanted one. I've never trusted anyone, or given a damn what anyone thinks."

"Why me?" I held my breath.

"Truthfully? I have no idea. You're different from anyone I've met before and I like your company." He hesitated a moment. "Please, come down. I'll even let you hold the torch."

Curiosity got the better of me, as did the thrill of being near him. I climbed down the ladder and took the torch from him. He stood still, gazing at me. Awkward with the silence, I scrambled for words. "You never did tell me if you can fly."

"I can't fly, but I can move faster than you can blink." He was gone! I swung the torch around and saw I was alone in a narrow corridor. I heard a laugh.

"If you're going to run off, I'm going back," I called. My nerves had caught up with me again.

"You did ask." In a flash, he was a few steps in front of me, walking backwards as he spoke. "I can jump much higher than humans, so I guess, combined with the speed, it could be mistaken with flight." He allowed me to draw level with him and turned to walk beside me, so close we were almost touching. "I'll show you sometime. Maybe on Exmoor where there's lots of space and when no one else is around. We could sit and watch the stars."

I shone the torch up to his grinning face. "Hmmm, we'll see. You might want to work on your chat-up lines."

We came to a place where the passage widened and there were two doorways.

Karl pointed to the door on the right. "That leads into the cellar under the house. You can't see the door from the other side; it's well hidden. Stairs lead from the cellar to the room you first met me in." He pointed down the passageway. "If you carry on, it takes you far away from the estate. Several of us had these tunnels built after the hunters tried burning houses down to trap us in daylight."

As he spoke, he pressed a code into a keypad, shielding it with his hand so I couldn't see. The door opened. I don't know what I expected, but it wasn't what I saw.

I stepped into a huge chamber that had been dug out and lined with stone. The surprise was that it looked more like a living room than a cave or tunnel. There was a massive chandelier hanging centrally, which cast a soft glow over the room, and the furnishings easily rivalled the main house in grandeur.

"Wow!" I looked around in wonder. "It's even warm in here."

"I brought down an electric heater. I don't feel the cold myself, but I thought you would."

"Very thoughtful, except you obviously assumed I would agree to come down here." I wasn't sure whether I should feel complimented or offended by him.

"No harm in being hopeful, and I'm glad you did agree."

"So you should be." I looked up at him with a half-smile. "I wouldn't usually follow men I hardly know down dark passageways."

Giving a slight bow, he grinned back at me. "I feel honoured."

I laughed. "Good. Can I ask you another question?"

He smiled. "I'm sure it must be my turn again."

He settled on the sofa and gestured with his hand for me to sit beside him.

I opted for an armchair, still keeping my distance. He looked totally relaxed, and I tried to do the same. "Okay, go on then. Ask your question."

"Why did your husband leave you?"

I was too stunned to answer for a moment. I couldn't believe Lord Ashton had spoken to him about it. "How do you know about that, and what business is it of yours anyway?"

"I heard you tell Tom."

"You sneak around the house, listening in. How sad is that."

"I do *not* sneak around."

"So how did you hear it?" I snapped. "I'm sure you weren't about to pop in to join us for a chat."

He sat up and drew in a long breath. There was nothing relaxed about him now.

I sank inside. "Why can't you trust me? What have I ever done?"

He stared for a moment. "Emily... I do trust you... more than any woman I've ever known."

"Huh. Sounds like it." I stared at the deep red rug on the floor, hoping he wouldn't notice the tears in my eyes.

"I put myself at risk for you. Or haven't you noticed?"

I turned my eyes on him. "What about the risk to me? You're a vampire, and I'm here alone with you, and all I can feel is how you don't trust me!"

He raised his chin. "Actually, you're not the only one with special sensitivities."

"Do you spy through key holes as well? Anyway, what special sensitivity?"

He looked about the room, then back to me. "Okay, I'll tell you. My senses are fine-tuned like your sensitivity to emotions. I hear everything in the house, whether I want to or not. I'm just thankful the house isn't still full of servants and their endless chatter and gossip driving me insane."

My mind desperately tried to remember all the conversations I'd had with Tom. *What exactly has he heard? He can't have heard anything very interesting, and I definitely haven't talked about him.* "It still isn't any of your business."

"No, but you can't expect me to answer your questions if you don't answer mine." He looked stern, but not angry.

He did have a point, and there were lots of things I wanted to ask him, so I told him the truth, or rather part of it.

"My husband decided he couldn't live with someone who didn't love him. I never lied to him or pretended I did. He knew from the start, but we both thought I would come to love him in time."

"Why did you get married? You must have been really young."

"I was eighteen and stupid. I thought I wanted marriage and children. I married someone placid, safe and totally boring. I wanted to make it work, and we got on most of the time, but I couldn't get pregnant. We talked about IVF, but I wasn't sure and he was against it. There just didn't seem any point in pretending after that."

"I should have left him, but I didn't have the strength. I've been in a pretty bad place for a while. I don't blame him for leaving me. I don't think I would have ever loved him. I'm not sure I'm capable of loving anyone." My eyes filled with tears as I remembered the pain of feeling useless.

He nodded. "That's something we have in common then. I'm not sure I'm capable of loving anyone either."

I blinked away my tears. "Did you ever love anyone before you were a vampire?"

He smiled, but his eyes looked sad. "I loved my son."

"I love my family; I didn't mean that sort of love." I tried to pick up his feelings, but was left with only my own. "Did you love your wife?

"No." He shook his head, then looked away. "I've never loved any woman... and that includes my family. My Mother was weak. She turned a blind eye to my Father's drunken beatings." His eyes returned to me, piercing through me, his nostrils flaring. "He beat her, and he beat me! I hated the whores he paraded in front of me. I hated my Mother for dying young and leaving me with him. Most of all, I hated my wife for taking my son away!"

I leant forward, wanting to be closer to him. His lips talked of anger, but his eyes talked of pain. "Tell me more."

For a moment, I thought I saw his eyes turn black, then he lowered his head. *Was it a trick of the light?* He stayed silent for a while, then stood and went to a nearby cabinet. He poured something into two glasses.

"A drink first," he said, holding out a glass. His eyes were a cool shade of green.

I gawped at the red liquid.

He laughed. "It's wine, not blood; don't worry."

"It's only mid-afternoon. What will Ned think if I go out smelling of drink? He probably wonders where I am already."

"Rubbish. He'll be having an afternoon nap after his lunch and a generous helping of scotch."

I shrugged and took a sip. It tasted good. I waited for him to speak.

He stared into the wine, turning the glass in his hand. "Marriage was expected back then and I knew the only way of getting Father to let me handle the estate was to get married and have a son."

"My wife's name was Catherine; she was the parson's daughter and the least annoying of prospective brides. Like you, I didn't lie; she knew I didn't love her, but I treated her with respect. I certainly wasn't cruel to her."

"Once she'd had Toby I kept out of her way most of the time. She had enough money to buy anything she wanted, my Father spent most of the time in his room asleep or in a local bar and I was happy running the business."

He paused and looked at me. "Do you really want to hear all this?"

I nodded "Yes. But only if you're happy to tell me."

He gave a weak smile. "Okay, but it isn't a happy tale. My Grandfather had done well in stocks and shares. Father managed to waste a lot of money on drink, but he hadn't touched the bulk of the assets."

"As I got older, he found he couldn't bully me anymore. One day, when I was nineteen, he went for me with the poker. I picked up a chair and threw it at him. He went down hard and banged his head. When he came around, I had tied his hands and feet together." He paused to sip from his wine glass.

I was perched on the edge of the chair. What kind of father attacks his son with a poker? It was beyond even my imagination. I was horrified, yet riveted. "What happened then?"

"I told him he either made me his partner, or the next time he got drunk I'd burn the house down with him in it."

"You said what?" *Surely, he hadn't meant it. Had he?* "Did he believe you?"

"Not at first. He laughed and said he'd kill me as soon as he got free." He stood and fetched the wine bottle, refilling his glass as he returned. He held out the bottle, but I shook my head. I'd hardly touched the first glass. It seemed to stick in my throat.

"I'm sorry, Karl."

He raised his eyebrows. "What for? It's hardly *your* fault."

"No, I know, but I can't even begin to understand what it was like for you. It must have been hell."

"It was, but I was determined not to let him win."

"What did you do?"

He looked at the floor and spoke in hushed tones. "I got some fuel from the garage and poured it around him. Then I lit a match."

My mouth hung open, speechless.

"I'm sorry, Emily. I know it sounds horrendous. And it was. But I'd spent my whole life being bullied by him. I was just trying to survive. I don't think I would have done it. Not then. But he must have thought I would. He agreed to the partnership, and we had it drawn up legally. Any major transactions had to have my signature as well as his, so he couldn't sell any of the estate without me. I bought land with most of the money left in the bank."

I closed my mouth and gulped back my emotions. Despite the danger, I was drawn to him, like a moth to a flame. "What about your wife?"

"I knew she was up to something because she started going into town more and she suddenly looked happier. I wasn't jealous, but I wasn't having her make a fool of me, so I followed her. I saw her go into the back of the bakery and followed. She was kissing the baker and giggling like a stupid schoolgirl. I was so angry I stormed straight in and punched him so hard he was out cold for several minutes."

"To be honest, it was my pride that she had hurt. I wasn't having her destroying my reputation, not after I'd worked so hard to try to restore the family name. It was bad enough my father had made himself a laughingstock to every landowner in the county; I wasn't having them gossip about my wife like she was a common whore. She whimpered and cried and blamed me for not caring about her."

"Well, you didn't, did you?"

"I didn't love her. But I had been as kind as I knew how to be. I thought she was happy with the way things were. She never said otherwise."

"Perhaps she simply couldn't live without love. Most people can't." I met his gaze with my own. Could he tell I was falling in love with him? Would he even care?

He gave me a lopsided smile. "I always thought love was overrated, but I'm beginning to wonder."

My heart banged against my chest. *What does he mean?* Afraid to ask, I diverted, "What happened to Toby. Can you tell me?"

He tipped the rest of his wine back his throat before replying. "The next day she took Toby into town and never came back." His pain ran through me like a knife. "How could she do that to me? I'd never hurt her. I know I wasn't the best husband, but I gave her everything she asked for. And I loved Toby. I was a good father." He looked at me intently, as if he needed me to understand the anguish she had put him through.

"It must have been awful." I knew it sounded weak, but I didn't know what else to say. It was enough to encourage him to continue.

"Early the next morning, I heard movement outside on the gravel. I looked out of the window and saw her climbing into the driver seat of one of the carriages. I knew she'd never driven horses, but there she was, thrashing the whip, trying to get away before I could stop her."

"I saw Toby's face pressed against the window of the carriage; the horses reared up and took off, charging along, scared to death of the flying whip. I threw on some clothes and raced out of the house. I ran after her, screaming for her to stop, but the horses were completely out of control. They veered off across the grounds and down a slope. I saw it all. She was thrown off, and the horses tore down over the rough ground with Toby inside the carriage. I watched as the horses swerved and the carriage broke loose from them. It...it rolled down the hill, rocking on its wheels, gaining speed... At the bottom, it crashed into a stone wall."

I waited, stunned, for him to go on.

I pulled Toby from the wreckage; his skull was smashed. I carried him home." He paused, looking away. I knew he was struggling with unbearable pain.

"Was she dead too?" I asked softly, clutching my glass tightly. I tried not to picture that poor child, covered in blood, but the deep red wine I was holding conjured up hideous images.

He turned towards me. "She was dying. I left her."

What could I say? No wonder there were no pictures of her. I looked at my wine in silence and then put the glass down. I felt sick. I got up and hovered there, I felt I should go, but I was reluctant to leave him. He wasn't letting me feel anything from him, but the pain was etched on his face.

I crouched by his chair. "I'm glad you told me, and I'm sorry you had to go through losing a child."

"Are you, really?" he said.

I thought I saw something in his eyes. Some warmth perhaps? Some connection?

"Yes, of course. No one deserves to lose a child like that. But why hold on to the anger towards your wife? It was a long time ago."

He looked up, his eyes boring into mine, only a few inches away. "Because it's better than hating myself."

For a moment, he let me feel his guilt mixed with pain, and I winced as it twisted inside of me.

"It was an accident, Karl. A tragic accident. It wasn't your fault. As for your wife... she paid the ultimate price. She lost her child and her life."

I took his hand and gripped it tightly in my own, wanting to share his pain, even though it could cripple me.

I recoiled so fast that I fell clutching my chest. My heart beat so quickly, I thought it would kill me. The pain tore through me as I gasped for air.

"What did you do?!" he cried, springing from the chair.

Why was he shouting at me? I'm in pain and he's shouting at me. "I didn't do anything," I rasped. I didn't have the energy to say more, and I couldn't think because his anger was coming through as intensely as his pain.

"Are you some sort of witch?" He spat the words at me.

I would have laughed at this if I hadn't been crying, tears of pain streaming down my face. I pulled in short, sharp, rapid breaths as my heart threatened to break free from my ribs. This was his pain. How did he manage to carry such a burden? He must have buried it, and I had somehow tapped into it and set it free. Now he blamed me, and I blamed me. What had I done? He was across the room as far as he could get with his fists clenched and his eyes burning red.

"I'm sorry," I said, scared of him and scared *for* him.

"What did you do?" he asked, more calmly this time, he was gaining composure.

"Nothing on purpose. It just happens."

I was recovering, pulling myself up. He kept well back, suspicion in his eyes. I pulled my legs towards my chest and sat hugging my knees; I was suddenly cold.

Then I told him how it was with me, how it had always been. I told him how I got nothing from him, and I had to know. It had never caused an adverse effect before, well only for me.

"Why would you care what I do or don't feel? I have spent decades trying not to feel. You talk about feelings being transferred to you, but this felt more like you tore them out from me. You should have left them buried."

"I could help you. I could take it."

"Take what?"

"The pain, the rage. I could take some of it."

He looked incredulous. "NO! Are you crazy? It would destroy you."

"And you care?" I wanted him to say yes, but he ignored my question.

"It would destroy both of us."

"We weren't expecting it this time; I could take it."

"Why would you do that? Never mind; just go. I can't be near you anymore."

He turned his back on me and waited silently. I picked up the torch and walked trembling to the door. *Why did I do that? Why do I feel a pain ripping my chest in two? Why do I want to help him?* I knew it made no sense, but I also knew I couldn't walk away forever. As soon as I was in the passage, I ran back to the woods, hardly able to see through the tears.

K4

December...

Four long weeks, and still no Karl. God, I missed him. I knew I shouldn't, but I did. However much he vexed me, he'd filled an empty hole in my life. He represented danger and excitement, but something more too. I recognised something in him that was broken; I longed to fix it, or at least try.

I couldn't get him out of my head. The way his green eyes pinned me to the spot; the way he singled me out. He seemed genuinely interested in me and it thrilled me; not because of his looks – which were pretty amazing- but because I knew he had given me his trust, and he didn't give it lightly. I was afraid he wouldn't trust me again, and I didn't think I could bare to work at the manor if he didn't.

I went through the motions. I worked; I went back to my friend's house; my work was great, and my friend was great. Her name is Holly and she's always been laid back and calm. Being with her soothed me.

Holly knew something was wrong. She thought it was my employer. I told her about Lord Ashton and she thought I fancied him. I let her think it. I also let her think he had upset me. I'd never been dishonest with her before, but what choice did I have?

Lord Ashton knew there was something wrong too. He thought it was *my* home life and that Holly had upset me.

It was a mess; a nightmare. I kept stopping at the portrait and looking at Karl's face, half hoping I could conjure him up if I stared long enough. I realised then that he's more than handsome, he's beautiful; a beautiful nightmare. I wished he were *my* beautiful nightmare.

It was early December, and the ground outside was frozen. Even with the central heating on, the large drawing room was cold. I learnt to light the open fire; it took the chill from the room, but not from my heart. I felt more at home in the manor than anywhere I had actually lived. *At least the house wants me.*

Outside, all the flowers had died, so I had cut holly each week and laid it on the tiny grave. It wasn't the child I mourned; it was Karl, and the child I'd never had.

I felt ridiculous. It wasn't the first time I'd fallen for someone unsuitable, and the result was always the same; heartache and pain. When I married, I thought only the love of a child could bring me back to life again. It wasn't to be. I looked at the faint scars on the insides of my arms. I felt ashamed of them now. They were self-inflicted reminders that there were still some things I could control.

I had thought I was through the worst, but I wasn't. There's something far worse than pain or suffering; there is nothing – the nothing that fills every day with emptiness, too heavy to carry – the nothing that shrivels your soul. I had almost resigned myself to nothing. Then there was the advert. Then there was the Manor. Then there was Karl. I thought there had been a reason for it all, that it was fate. I'd really believed I was strong enough to help him.

I wept with the emptiness I felt.

Only three weeks until Christmas, and I was dreading it. Lord Ashton was going to visit family in Kent, Ned would be staying with his granddaughter in Cornwall, and Holly was going to her parents' house. I'd been invited to my parents, along with my brother and his wife.

Normally this wouldn't present a problem. Normally I would look forward to it. Normal had nothing to do with my life anymore.

If only there was someone I could talk to. If only there was someone who would understand. Loving Karl left me isolated from the rest of my world. And he didn't seem to care.

For four days, the manor would be closed up and I would have to play happy families at my parents' with a smile on my face, and a pain in my heart. It would be torture. I wasn't even that close to my brother. It wasn't that I didn't love him, I would soon jump to his defence if anyone else criticised him, but I didn't understand him, and he certainly didn't understand me.

I remember telling my brother I wasn't really his sister. I was seven; he was four. Even then he thought I was crazy. I didn't feel like I belonged in the same family; I still don't.

The only way I could think of to survive was to tell myself I didn't care about Karl. I went shopping and bought presents. I went out with friends and drank too much. I tried not to think about him. I tried.

And then one day, while cleaning the study, I felt something. I felt wisps of uncertainty and confusion that weren't mine.

I knew it was him before I turned. My feelings spiralled. I was so glad I could have run to him and kissed him, yet so angry at him for disappearing I could have slapped his face. I found I couldn't do either; I was frozen to the spot. I stood and waited for him to speak.

"I wanted to see if you were okay."

I fought back a rush of tears. "I'm fine; why shouldn't I be?"

His eyes searched mine. "You're angry with me."

"Yes, I am! You pop in and out of my life when it suits you, and I don't want to be part of your game anymore."

His eyes held mine. "I didn't come here to play games."

"Then why did you come here?" I felt my anger dissolving. I wanted to reach out to him, but fear kept me still.

"Because I missed you. Don't ask me to explain why, or how I feel, because I don't have a clue. I've spent too many years not feeling anything. I wanted to get away and bury everything again. I wanted to forget I ever met you. Then I remembered how dull my existence was before you were here. I don't know what to do."

"Neither do I," I cried.

"How do you cope?"

"Not very well most of the time, but I would rather be hurt than feel nothing."

I found myself walking towards him and stretching my arms out, wanting to take his hands in mine, but I stopped, remembering the last time I touched him.

He looked at my bare arms, then his eyes met mine again.

"Those scars... did you do that?"

I quickly pulled my sleeves down and nodded, embarrassed. "Like I told you, I was in a bad place for a while. I'm stronger now."

"Good. I don't want anything like that to happen again, and I don't want you wasting tears on me." He spoke softly and I'm sure the green of his eyes changed. They looked softer; less cool.

"I meant what I said before," I told him. "Let me help you. I'm stronger than I look."

"I'm sure you are, but what about me? What if you take away the anger and pain and there's nothing left. What if that's all I can feel?"

"If you really believed that, you wouldn't be here."

He walked over to the desk and sat on it facing the window. It was a dull miserable day, with no chance of sunlight entering the room.

"You know it won't change what I am, don't you?" He turned to look at me with concern. I could still feel his confusion, but I wasn't confused anymore. I had been right all along. I was needed here.

I nodded and sat on the desk next to him, careful to leave a gap so that we weren't touching. He put his fist on his lap, only inches away from where my hand was resting and then crooked his little finger out and smiled.

I hooked my little finger through his and raised my eyebrows in question. "Friends?"

He smiled. "It's a good place to start anyway."

There was no jolt of pain this time. I knew he was blocking most of it from me, but not everything. I still had to grit my teeth as his pain washed over me, but there was something else too. Something good. I looked out across the lawn to the rain-laden trees and said softly, "I missed you too."

That was the first time I felt something good from him. It was so tiny it hardly existed at all and he was very quick to hide it again, but it didn't matter because I knew it was there.

We sat like that for a while, silently together, allowing the pain to wash over us.

It soon became a routine. Karl would appear while Lord Ashton was out and we would talk. Sometimes, he would make me laugh with tales of the things he had seen; sometimes he made me want to cry. One day, he even picked up a duster to help, but I laughed and asked him if he knew how it worked, so he threw it down and picked me up in his arms, spinning me around until I was laughing and giddy.

Sometimes he would sit and hold his little finger out for me to take and he would share a little of what he felt. It hurt, but that was okay. I felt like I had found my purpose. It's hard to explain, but when he showed me his fear and pain, allowed me to see his vulnerability, I felt stronger. He trusted me, and that was special.

I didn't ask him any more questions for a while; I listened. He always thanked me and made me feel appreciated. I realised our relationship wasn't balanced. He had all the physical power, money and status, while I was merely the cleaner. All I can say is; he did nothing to make me feel that way. He made me feel special. He made me feel like I was the only person in the world who could reach him. The fact that he was dangerous just added a thrill to our meetings.

Sometimes, I thought I felt something positive from him, but he always shut it down so fast that I was left doubting its existence. I wasn't sure if he could ever love me, but he made me feel like he needed me. It made me feel powerful.

I was leading a double life. My family and friends noticed that I was suddenly happier. They all thought there was something between Lord Ashton and me. He was treating me more like a friend every day and less like a servant. He asked me to call him Tom, but it didn't seem right. Especially as I was deceiving him right under his nose.

I lived for the moments with Karl. Only our fingers had touched, yet I was more aware of his body close to mine than I'd been of any man's before. I was more aware of my own body than I had ever been before.

I was also aware of my feelings. I knew I was falling in love.

Eventually, my curiosity got the better of me and I asked him; "How did you become a vampire?"

Lord Ashton had gone into town for something, I was peeling vegetables with the blind down, and the spotlights on, Karl was part watching me and part reading the paper. It was amazing how fast he filled in every crossword. When I commented on it, he just shrugged and said he had plenty of time to pick up useless information. We had been chatting about things in the news, but when I asked him my question, he folded the paper and looked at me.

"You don't have to tell me if you don't want to," I added quickly.

"I don't mind telling you, but if you ask me questions, please be prepared to hear things you don't like."

"I already know you're a vampire. How much worse can it get?"

"You don't understand, Emily. I was out of control, for many years. I caused complete carnage and I enjoyed it."

I looked at him wide-eyed and open-mouthed, trying to match the horror in my head with the man before me. I felt like I should probably hate him, or, at least be too horrified to want him near me. I wasn't sure how my heart could love him, but it did.

"I'm not proud of the things I have done, but I want you to know the truth. I want to know if you can care for me despite everything."

"Then tell me. It's okay, I know what you are and I accept it."

"I can't decide if you're mad or amazing!"

"Go on, tell me what happened." Could he think I was amazing? I pretended to ignore the comment, but I was secretly thrilled. I sat at the table opposite him so that I could listen properly. I was nervous as I waited for him to talk, hoping I could keep my promise and accept whatever he told me.

"After Toby's death, I went crazy. I started going to bars just to get drunk. I got into fights, but people were lenient because of who I was, and because they knew I had just lost a son. I wanted to be punished. I hated myself for letting my son die. Blaming my wife only helped for a while. I was so filled with rage, I wanted to take on the whole world."

"One night, I was in a bar out of town, sitting in a corner looking into an empty glass. A man sat opposite me and told me he could help. He asked me how I'd like to be feared and respected forever. I was sceptical of course, I hadn't met him before and had no idea how he knew about me. His name was Benedikte. When I asked him how he could help me, he offered to show me."

He stopped and frowned, seeming unsure how to continue. I guessed he was wondering how much to tell me.

"Go on, It's okay... I promise." I reached out and put my hand over his. He didn't pull away, but I knew he was guarding his feelings.

He avoided my gaze as he continued, "I followed him upstairs where he had a room at the Inn. There was a girl tied to a chair, another to the bed. I told him I wasn't interested in cheap whores. I'd seen enough of them through my father; they disgusted me.

I thought they were drugged, because they didn't say a word or call out, but when he knelt near one of them, she actually smiled like she was pleased to see him. I thought for a minute he expected me to watch him having sex with her and went to leave, but he called for me to wait and said he had something important to show me. Then he bit her.

The crazy thing was that she seemed to welcome it. I was shocked. I had no idea then what he was, but I was rooted to the spot. I watched as he drank from her, he didn't kill her; just left her helpless. I wanted that power, so I asked him to help me."

I felt a deep weariness in him that made me ache. My own feelings were confused. He spoke one minute with sadness, the next with venom. I didn't want to hear more, but I had to.

"How did it happen? What did he do?"

"You've seen the movies. He bit me; I had to drink his blood." He suddenly sounded flippant, but I wasn't fooled.

"Is it really that simple?"

"No, there is nothing simple about it, believe me. He drank my blood until I was unconscious and my heart stopped beating. I was dead to this world. Then I was dragged up from hell by his blood and his breath."

It sounded like some hideous form of CPR. I couldn't even begin to imagine the full horror of it. I gripped his hand in both of mine, wishing I could save him from his anguish.

"It must have been agony."

"It hurt like nothing I'd ever felt before."

I felt the sharp pain just before he pulled his hand away.

"Please don't do that," I whispered.

"Do what?"

"Shut me out. You want me to trust you. Trust me back."

He avoided my eyes and looked down at his hands, shifting sideways in the chair at the same time.

"I don't want to hurt you", he muttered quietly.

"I know and like I said, I trust you."

"Maybe you shouldn't." He looked at me now, deadly serious.

"What!" Why was he saying this now? "You wanted me to trust you. Remember? You sought my company, not the other way around." I sounded cross, but I was hurt. It felt like he was messing me about.

"That was before." He was avoiding my gaze.

"Before what?"

"Before I gave a shit!" He looked at me now, eyes blazing. I couldn't pick up what he was feeling because he was still blocking, but he seemed angry more than anything else. I didn't know what to think. I wanted him to care about me, but not to hate me for it too.

"Why does that have to be a bad thing?" I said more softly; I really didn't want him to run from it.

"Because I don't have the slightest idea what to do with anything that's good." He looked so troubled, I wanted to reach out to him, but stopped myself.

"I happen to give a shit too you know!" I said, smiling.

For a moment, he grinned, then his face darkened again. "Look, there are only three ways this can go." He spoke sternly.

"Which are?"

"One- we have sex, start a relationship, and are happy for a while. Not necessarily in that order."

"Glad to hear it. And the other two?"

I was shocked at the mention of sex, but the thrill that ran through my body was undeniable. I realised I was gripping the table.

"Two-we have sex, attempt a relationship, it fails and we hate each other."

God, what chance did we have if he had already decided it was doomed? I tried to sound flippant, "Can't say I like that idea much." My heart was hammering hard. *He must be able to hear it.*

"Three- we stay friends, in which case you really need to let me block some of my feelings towards you, and I should probably walk out of this room now."

I didn't answer straight away and he took this to mean I wanted him to go. He got up and walked towards the door. The truth was I did know what I wanted, but I was afraid to say it.

"Friends it is then," he said, keeping his back to me.

"Is that what you want? I notice you mentioned sex, but not love."

He turned to face me. "Look, I'm trying to do the right thing for once in my miserable existence. I wouldn't know the first thing about relationships, not positive ones anyway. Do I think I could love you? Yes. But I can't promise anything, and I don't want to screw your life up."

"I'm quite capable of doing that all on my own and I'm certainly no expert where relationships are concerned." I got up and took a step toward him. I knew I was taking a risk, but

I believed he could love me. "Please just tell me what you want."

He moved closer, fixing me with his green eyes. "Right now, I want to kiss you."

My breath stopped for a moment, but I mustered a smooth response. "Then you should have just asked."

In a split second, he had pulled me to his chest and I felt, with surprise, that he had a slow, but steady heartbeat. I could also feel hard muscle and the strength of his arms around me. Every part of me tingled with anticipation as his eyes searched my face. Then his lips were on mine and I was lost in him.

It was like cold air hitting hot and causing a storm deep inside me. He easily lifted me with one hand, so that our faces were level. He buried the other hand in my long hair and twisted it at the back of my neck. I let out a small moan of pleasure. He let his guard slip a bit so I could feel his passion above the pain and anger.

Another feeling reached from his heart to mine. It wasn't love, but it was good. He cared for me and that was enough right then. I gasped as he pulled away too soon.

"Dear Thomas has returned I'm afraid; I can hear the car out the front. I'd better go." He kissed me on the cheek and held me at arm's length for a moment. "I take it we're going for option one," he whispered. His breath in my ear made me shudder.

"Go! He'll be in here any minute." I laughed, not really wanting him to go anywhere.

"Not until you answer." He was teasing now. It was all I could do not to giggle like a child.

"Okay, but not necessarily in that order!"

He did a mock bow and disappeared from the room. I was left flustered and short of breath, but happy, very happy.

For the rest of the week, I was on cloud nine. Karl kept appearing while I was working. We talked, we kissed and he held me like I was the most precious thing he'd ever discovered.

I worked really hard and fast most of the day, so that Lord Ashton – Tom, I must remember to call him Tom – didn't notice that little work got done while he was out of the house. I was amazed he didn't wonder what was going on when I looked so hot and flustered, but he seemed to think I had been working too hard and insisted I sit down for a drink! I did feel guilty then. He had been good to me and I was betraying him.

The feelings Tom gave off had become much more positive over the last few weeks and I wondered if he had found a girlfriend. I asked Karl about it; because I was surprised he was single.

"Tom's far too scared to bring girlfriends near me!" Karl said with scorn. Noticing my horrified face, he continued. "I didn't say he had reason to be afraid. He's a coward. If he stood up to me, I might respect him more. Not that I really want him having a wife in the house, but I suppose it will be necessary to carry on the name, and the business."

We were sitting next to each other on the living room floor. It was too cold for me in the old servant's quarters, but Ned was gardening close to the house, so I didn't dare close the curtains completely. We had laughed like kids as we crawled across the floor and behind the sofa, avoiding the sunlight and the possibility of Ned seeing us. Now I wondered why Tom was so complacent about leaving me alone. I asked Karl for his thoughts.

"I haven't been completely honest with him about my tolerance of daylight. He thinks I wouldn't dare come above ground before it gets completely dark. That's why he insists you go so early. If he knew the truth he'd have a fit." He grinned and kissed my neck, sending fear and excitement through me in equal measures.

One day, I wondered aloud how the house and business had ended up being passed to Tom. Karl was hovering around me, deliberately distracting me from my work. Not that I minded.

"I don't get it."

"Get what?" he replied. "How to dust a table while I'm kissing your ear?"

I turned around and flicked him with the duster, laughing.

"Oh, is that what it was? I thought it was an annoying fly."

"Don't be cruel!" He tried to look serious, but I could feel he was laughing inside.

"I was wondering how Tom ended up here."

"Tom now, is it?"

I'm not saying he was jealous, but I definitely detected annoyance. "Don't be ridiculous, he insisted on me calling him that and he's only being friendly."

He snorted, but said nothing.

I returned to the subject. "I guess he lives here because you didn't have more children after Toby."

"No, being a vampire did make things complicated. It wasn't so much the name I cared about then, but running the business. I needed someone who could look like they were running things, so that meetings could be conducted in daylight. I also wanted to let people think I was dead after a few years, before they noticed I wasn't aging.

I eventually left a note, so that the locals thought I'd gone off to commit suicide. The police were pretty stupid back then; they didn't question it too much. My Father didn't realise I knew, but he had made one of the women in the village pregnant. The boy was four when Toby died. The stupid girl was only too happy to accept my promises of legitimacy and marriage to my Father. I persuaded a priest to marry them while Father was too drunk to notice what was happening."

I was shocked by his cruelty, but I was so in love with him and so interested in everything about him, I didn't show it. "How did you get the priest to agree to that?"

"Let's just say he did more than say prayers with one of the altar boys. Anyway, Father met with an unfortunate accident soon afterwards, as did the priest. The mother died as soon as the boy was old enough to be useful."

"You killed them all." It was a statement, not a question. His words tore through me like shards of ice.

"Yes, except the boy. His name was Robert. I never liked him, he was weak and easy to manipulate. He knew I hadn't killed myself but was too scared to say anything. I hired a governess for appearances, but taught him everything myself. She didn't talk because I showed her what I could do if she did."

I felt uneasy. Either he was blocking me again or he really did feel nothing for them. "And now I'm being weak and easy to manipulate." I looked down at my feet, finally realising just how big a risk I was taking.

"No, Emily, you're giving me a chance to be different; better." He lifted my chin with his fingertips. "I am telling you about the man I was. I don't want it to be who I am now."

"Karl, I..."

He silenced me with his lips and feelings, which he allowed me to feel completely. As I melted into his desire, passion and lust, I picked up that vibe again, but stronger now. It felt like something growing in him; it felt like love.

K5

It was two days until Christmas. Tom was in a flap, preparing to visit his family. He hadn't even wrapped any of his presents. He *had* bought a new trailer for his beloved mares, so they could go with him.

It was easy to see why he made such a fuss of his horses; they were beautiful. A chestnut called Jenna and a grey called Gem. Apparently – according to Ned – they were worth a bob or two. I had only watched them from a distance, but I admired the grace with which they moved when they galloped through their field, or walked, heads high, when led. I longed to touch them, but I was afraid to ask. After all, I was just the cleaner.

I took pity on Tom and offered to wrap all the presents. He was planning to travel that afternoon and return the day after Boxing Day. We managed to get everything sorted out ready for the house to be closed up by lunch time. I insisted he should eat before he left, and I made sandwiches. I fussed around him, delaying his departure, but in truth, I was hoping to see Karl.

The last time I'd seen Karl, he had made it quite clear he didn't celebrate Christmas. He thought it was a waste of time and money. But I still wanted to say goodbye before I left for four days. My chest felt tight with anxiety as I tried to think of a way to see him. I hated how much it mattered to me. I felt needy and vulnerable, like a child. *Was he thinking of me?*

Tom's voice broke through my thoughts. "How did I ever manage before you came here, Emily?"

"I often wonder that myself, Tom," I said, laughing with a carelessness I didn't feel, "but I'm not intending to go anywhere, so you won't have to." I had grown rather fond of him in a sisterly sort of way.

"Good. I have a small gift for you. It's nothing much, but I wanted to say thank you. You don't know how much easier my life has been since you came."

He seemed very pleased with himself, as he handed me a small box. It was badly wrapped, but I loved the fact that he had tried. I could feel his nerves as he waited for me to open it.

"Thank you, but you shouldn't have. It's me who should be thanking you." I wondered if I had misread Tom. Was he just being friendly? I felt so many emotions inside, it was hard to separate his from my own.

Inside the little box was a pair of gold earrings. They had small droppers with what looked like rubies in them.

"I hope you like them. I thought red would suit you."

"They're lovely. Thanks." I was thrilled and decided to take it as a friendly gesture. It was nice to be appreciated.

We said our goodbyes, and I went through towards the back of the house to get my bag and coat. As I passed the door of the old servants' quarters, something grabbed my arm. I gasped as I was pulled sideways into a room.

"What are you playing at?" I was startled, as the white-hot heat of rage burst into my chest. Looking into Karl's red-tinged eyes, I knew the feeling was his. Confused, I pushed the feeling away, only for it to be replaced by shards of jealousy piercing my head and ripping at my throat. I gasped and clutched at my collar, trying to loosen it, trying to breathe.

"What did he give you?" Karl growled, his face inches from mine.

I sighed, relieved, despite his anger. If that was all it was, I could easily explain. I was secretly pleased that he cared. "I assume this is about Tom giving me a small Christmas present. It's only a thank you for my work."

His eyes were narrowed, his voice cruel. "Don't be naive. What did he give you?"

My heart sinking, I fought off his feelings and tried to defend myself. *How dare he?* "It's none of your business and I'm not having you bully me. Let me go!" I reacted with anger, but panic was rising in me, like icy fingers, plucking at every nerve.

What would he do? What if Tom came past and heard us? What if I'd completely imagined Karl's feelings for me? No! I swallowed hard, trying to push my doubt back down, away from my head. I couldn't have imagined it. I squared my shoulders and stared back at him defiantly.

He let go of my arm but stayed angry. He lowered his voice to a whisper, his eyes still boring into me. "I heard you two laughing and joking. I think you care more for him than me."

He was trying to block his feelings from me, but something in the way he hung his head slightly and the way his voice caught as he spoke told me; *he's as afraid of losing me as I am of losing him.* I reached out to touch him, then stopped, still unsure.

I spoke softly, "Karl, I sneak around behind his back to see you. I don't care about anyone more than you."

He turned towards me slightly but said nothing.

"Look" I held out the earrings. "He gave me these. I can't really give them back now can I? He'll wonder why. Besides, I like them."

"And you like him."

"Yes, as a friend, period. I have to go before he wonders where I am, but I don't want to leave things like this."

He turned and looked at me directly, eyes challenging. "Come and see me over Christmas."

His words sounded like a demand, but I felt his uncertainty. Unsure what to do, I avoided answering directly. "You know

I'm out with Holly tomorrow, and staying with my parents over Christmas."

"Please?" He caught hold of my arm, but more gently this time." As his eyes softened, I became aware of a sliver of fear running up my arm from where he held it.

I smiled, placing my hand over his. "Maybe boxing day. I'll see."

"I told you. I'm not used to relationships. Give me a chance." He stroked the side of my face with his fingertips, allowing me into his feelings completely. His fear gripped my heart, making it ache.

"Okay, but you need to let me go now." I squeezed his hand, then turned to go.

"Take these." He shoved something into the pocket of my cardigan.

I quickly ran from the room and grabbed my things.

Once outside, I waved goodbye to Tom, then sat in my car. I reached into my pocket and removed an envelope. It was too heavy to be a letter. I tore it open and discovered two large keys. I recognised them as being the same as the keys Tom used. One was tagged, front gate – and the other, front door.

On Boxing Day afternoon, I was sitting on my bed in Holly's house, staring at the wall. It was a nice enough room and I knew I was lucky to be living with a friend like Holly. There was nothing exciting about my bedroom, certainly nothing about the wall I was staring at. It was an avoidance tactic because I knew the keys to Kenwood Manor lay in the drawer beside the bed and I was trying to pretend I didn't want to use them.

I knew that going to see Karl alone would be some sort of commitment on my part. There was no doubting I wanted to see him, but the strength of his jealousy had scared me.

I'd enjoyed the last two days more than I imagined I would. Holly and I had walked to a local pub for a drink Christmas Eve and met up with some other friends. I took quite a bit of stick about being "well in with the lord of the Manor", but I laughed it off.

I spent Christmas Day at my parents' house. I was wondering if I could manage the last mouthful of Christmas pudding, when my brother suddenly clinked his glass with a knife edge, then stood up.

"I have some good news to announce." He looked at his beaming wife, Donna, "We're having a baby!"

Everyone gasped and leapt up to congratulate them. I was filled with joy as I hugged each of them, yet part of me could have cried. They would have everything I wanted – a family.

Is it still what I want? I asked the bedroom wall. *Would a child really make me happy?*

Moving my gaze to the drawer by my bed, I realised. There was no decision to make. I'd made it the first time I'd seen Karl, and whether I like it or not, I was already committed.

Jumping from the bed, I threw open the wardrobe doors. I spent a ridiculous amount of time deciding what to wear. I tipped my underwear drawer out onto the bed and rummaged through an array of knickers and bras, trying to decide. Too drab... too tarty... yuck too grey and worn. I finally settled for a pale blue set that was pretty but not too outrageous, then pulled on a red jersey dress that Holly had given me, but I'd never worn.

Downstairs, I put on a long black winter coat and tucked the manor keys into my pocket. Pulling on my gloves, I went to the door reasonably satisfied with my appearance. My heart racing at the thought of seeing Karl, I ran back upstairs on impulse and threw in my makeup bag, toothbrush and toothpaste. *Best to be prepared!*

Outside, the darkness was descending and bringing the cold night air with it. I set off in my car, stalled it twice in the first fifty yards, calmed myself and managed the rest of the drive smoothly.

At the manor gates, I jumped out of the car, leaving the engine running, and switched my torch on. Shining the light at the big iron gates, I soon twisted the key in the lock and swung them open. Leaping back into the car, I drove through, then relocked the gate.

By the time I'd crunched along the gravel drive and parked outside the front of the house, my breaths were coming short and sharp. *What if he's changed his mind about me? What if he was just teasing me and I'm making an idiot of myself?*

I took several long slow breaths as I stepped from the car and approached the front porch. The house loomed above me in total darkness, then I felt him. Behind me. My body flooded with relief and joy.

I spun around, already knowing he was thrilled to see me. All my panic melted in an instant, and I smiled, though I could barely make out his features in the dusk. This man, who was usually far too sure of himself, was here and glad to see me.

"Let's go for a walk." He took my bag, ran up the front steps, and placed it inside the door.

"Okay, why not?" I was glad to walk beside him in silence. It gave me time to steady my breath and my feelings. It was cold but dry and the moon was almost full, so I could see quite well. The grounds looked so different in the dark. By day they were magnificent, the flowers and neatly clipped hedges gave way to more rugged woodland where the sun dripped from the branches into the stream. By night it looked magical, strange shapes cast by moonlight, the house looking ghostlike in the pond's reflection. I was enchanted, both by my surroundings and my escort.

I was glad I had worn boots and my warm coat, although I scarcely noticed the cold with Karl by my side.

He held out his arm for me to take, which I did with a giggle.

"And what may I ask is so amusing?"

"You are; I didn't know you could be such a gentleman, but I'm not complaining."

"Good. Have you enjoyed your time off so far?"

"Yes, thanks." I didn't say more because he was blocking his feelings. I wasn't sure if he was asking out of politeness or because he was hoping I had been miserable without him.

"So where did you go with Holly Christmas Eve?"

I became suspicious. *Is this the Spanish inquisition?* Then a little annoyed. I stopped, let go of his arm and turned to face him. "Why don't you just ask whatever it is you really want to know?"

Silence.

"I know you're blocking me, which probably means you think I've been flirting with other men or something, which by the way is insulting."

"That isn't why I was asking you; calm down. Don't you think you're being unfair? I can't tell what *you're* feeling, so why shouldn't I be able to keep my feelings to myself if I want to?"

I saw him frowning in the moonlight. "You could ask me how I feel if you want to know."

"So could you. You just don't trust me to tell the truth, which, by the way, I find insulting."

I realised he had a point. "Okay, I'm sorry. We went to The Flying Pig. It was fun, I saw some friends I hadn't seen for a while."

He remained quiet for a bit as we carried on walking up a small gravel path. We came to the summerhouse and I looked around at the tiny lights of the town below and up at the twinkling stars in the inky sky. I hadn't realised before how beautiful the night could be. I was a creature of the sunshine; this was his world, but I knew I could grow to like it. The universe suddenly seemed so much bigger as I stood there, and I felt very small. I didn't want to feel alone.

"Will you tell me what you are thinking?" I asked him softly.

He put his arm around my shoulder and turned to face me. "I was thinking that people in relationships normally go out to pubs and restaurants or the cinema or theatre. I was wondering if you wanted me to take you out somewhere. Not a restaurant, though, that would be a bit awkward as I don't eat."

It was a sharp reminder of his feeding habits, but even so, I was relieved. He'd been worrying about making me happy. "Is that all? I thought it was something serious."

He frowned and I quickly realised that he probably hadn't found it easy to tell me his thoughts, so I really should take it seriously. "I just mean that you don't need to worry. I like going out with my friends and I intend to carry on doing so, but I like coming here too. It's my favourite place in the world. You don't need to take me anywhere."

"Really?"

The pleasure he felt filled me too. "Really. Maybe someday we will want to go somewhere else for a change, but who needs the theatre with a view like that?"

He pulled me to him and kissed my hair. I would have been happy to stay there, but the night was getting colder and I couldn't help shivering.

He gave me a squeeze. "Come on; let's go back to the house, I've lit the fire in the lounge."

"I had no idea you knew *how* to light the fire in the lounge." I teased.

"I'm not completely useless you know." As he said this, he swept me up in his arms, and the world rushed past me so fast that it felt like I was at the front door of the house before I had even left the summerhouse.

"My heart was thumping so hard against my chest that he must have been able to hear it. "Do you think you could warn me before you do anything like that again?" I pulled a frown, but he knew I wasn't angry.

He opened the door without putting me down and carried me into the hall whilst kissing me. When he put me on my feet, I felt giddy. He took my coat and I sat to take my boots off. Before I had the chance, he was back, his fingers on the zipper of my right boot, slowly sliding it down, his eyes not leaving mine. Having discarded my boots he picked me up again and carried me to the lounge, turning sideways to push the door open with his shoulder. The room was warm and glowed with the reflection of amber flames.

"Hello, Karl. I see you've started the fun without me."

I heard the voice before I saw her. It was a voice that purred, but held no emotion. I twisted my neck to see a tall woman emerge from the shadows. I knew at once that she was a vampire. For one thing, she gave off no feelings and for another, no human could possibly look that gorgeous.

I felt a spike of anger and alarm from Karl as he swiftly put me down.

"Ana! What are you doing here?"

So, this was Ana. Her hair hung in dark ringlets to her tiny waist, pale skin emphasising dark lips and brown eyes. Smiling, she walked towards Karl, her hips swaying from side to side like a cobra; she was mesmerising.

As she approached, I moved aside.

She came right up to Karl and breathed in his face. "What do you mean? I always come over when Tom is away." She ran a cherry red nail down his chest then looked at me.

I felt sick.

"I see you brought me a Christmas present." She stepped up to me and looked me up and down. "Not your usual type, but I guess she's quite pretty."

I cringed as she touched my face and then my hair and I saw his muscles tense. *Who does she think she is, and why the hell don't you tell her to go?* In my head, I was shouting, but the words would not come out of my mouth. My eyes filled with tears and I willed my legs to move, but I was frozen. Still he said nothing. I looked from her to him and back again.

"Oh dear, I don't think she's ready for our kind of party. Where did you find her?"

Surely, this is where he would stand up for me and tell her to go. He looked from me to her as if undecided about what to say or do. His feelings cut off; he shut me out again.

"She's the cleaner."

And that's when my heart sank. It lay like a stone in the pit of my stomach, waiting for her cherry red nails to rip it right out of me. I'd walked straight into a nest of vipers. I'd trusted him and it had all been a lie.

She laughed. It was the cruellest laugh I've ever heard. I hated her. I hated him. I hated myself more. Why was I still standing there? I should be running, running away from them both.

"The hired help!" she hissed. "You have got to be kidding. Did you really get that lonely without me?"

She turned her cold smile on me. "Don't look so sad, lovey. You can go if you want."

I did want, so why the hell wasn't I moving?

Her eyes flashed between him and me. "Tell her she can go Karl; you don't need her now I'm here and she doesn't want to join in. Look at her."

He didn't look. He just said; "You had better go."

It was too much. I turned and ran from the room. Something flashed by me, and she was at the front door before I got to it, a cruel smile on her face.

"I've done you a favour. You wouldn't have lived until morning; they never live until morning."

"Ana!" Karl shouted behind me.

At last, he wants to silence her, but it's too late. "Who are *they*? *Who* doesn't live until morning?" I was afraid to find out, so why was I asking her?

"His lovers, the human ones. They don't have a very good shelf life, poor dears."

She is a snake and she is enjoying this. Am I her prey or is Karl?

"I bet sweet Thomas doesn't know you're here."

"Ana, that's enough. Let her go."

She stood aside and I fumbled with the doorknob. I gasped as I got outside and realised I'd been holding my breath, wondering if they would release me.

I wasn't safe yet.

I bolted to my car and realised my keys were still in my coat inside the house. For a moment, my mind froze, and my heart hammered in my chest. The door slammed and I turned to see my coat lying on the doorstep.

I ran and grabbed it. Thank goodness, car keys were in my pocket and so were the keys to the gate.

Pain sliced through my head and my chest. I curled tighter into a ball, as words drifted around me.

"Emily!"

Holly's voice? Where am I? A shiver ran up my spine. I was lying on something cold.

"Emily, what's wrong? Why are you on the floor?"

Her words meant nothing. I only knew pain. I couldn't think; I couldn't speak. I was aware she was trying to move me, and my body began to respond. Soon I lay softly on a bed. My bed? What had happened? A memory was stirring inside me, darker than onyx. I pushed it away, afraid to let it take hold of me.

Exhausted, I slept.

K6

Voices drifted into my room through the open door, gradually penetrating my awareness. My mind felt like it was gripped by cold damp fingers, pulling my thoughts inward to my broken heart. I was faintly aware that, somewhere outside of my body, Holly was talking to my parents. I groaned, praying the earth would swallow me whole. I couldn't feel their worry. I was too broken inside to feel anything except the deep sadness seeping into every pore of my body. No one could help me; I was alone with my pain.

"She hasn't eaten for three days, and I can't get her to talk to me. I don't know what to do." Normally, Holly's stress would cut through me, but the darkness was too heavy, too all consuming.

I vaguely heard Mum talking about my brother and his wife expecting a baby. Her voice lowered, but I knew she was wondering if I was in a state because of it. I could hear Dad vaguely mumbling, and then I caught Mum's words, "... not able to have her own baby..."

These words pierced the gloom for a moment, causing a sharp twist of pain somewhere deep in my gut. I whimpered like a wounded animal. Their words continued, gradually getting closer outside the door. I squeezed my puffy eyes tighter together. *Please make them go away.*

I heard Mum say something about getting medical help. Alarm shot through me. *No way! No doctors! I'll be fine!*

I knew they were about to enter the room. I tried to brace myself, ready for their anguish before they entered the room, but in my weakened state, I was helpless. Bile rose in my throat.

"Oh Emily," Mum cried, grabbing my hand.

I peered through the slits of my eyes. Large shapes hovered over me as I tried to make my brain work. Say something! It screamed at me. They may go away if you say something. I opened my mouth, hoping my detached mind would find something suitable.

"I'm so sorry," said my mouth, somewhere in the distance.

Dad leant over and kissed my forehead. "Don't worry love. Just rest. We'll come and see you again tomorrow.

Alone, I slept for the rest of the day and through the night.

Mid-morning, I woke, knowing I had to get myself mobile if only to pacify others. My parents would be visiting; I had to show I was improving.

I folded the duvet back and sat on the side of the bed, staring, wishing I could cry. Somehow, my mind took some control over my body. I dressed, pottered to the bathroom, and brushed my teeth. I stood over the basin, wondering how my heart would ever begin to heal. Downstairs, Holly had left notes for me saying there was chicken salad wraps in the fridge and she would see me later. I switched on the TV and was distantly aware of the flickering screen.

The doorbell jarred me out of my stupor. Pumped up with several deep breaths, I plodded down the hall and let my parents and their anxiety in.

"Are you feeling better?" Mum asked, studying me. "Have you eaten?"

"You need to rest," said Dad, his face full of strain.

I smiled and kissed them, then led them to the lounge. I perched on the sofa, trying to remember how I would have sat, had I still been whole.

Dad nestled close to me and took my hand in his. His anxiety washed over me; a welcome distraction from the gloom. "Is this about that Lord Ashton bloke?"

"No, he hasn't done anything wrong." I was surprised my voice sounded normal, calm even. Dad was looking at me expectantly, but what could I tell him? How could I explain that my insides had turned to lead, and each breath seemed like a waste of time? How could I explain the feeling that someone had switched off my life support, leaving me struggling to breathe?

My poor tired mind grasped at lucid thought. Some of Holly's words came back to me. She had noticed my bag was missing. I had dodged her questions, unable to answer truthfully, unable to face lying. But lie, I must.

"I went for a walk on my own after having a couple of drinks. I was attacked by someone and he stole my bag." I paused and looked at their open mouths. Their fear crept up my spine, and I welcomed its intrusion. "It scared me, but I'll be okay," I tried to reassure them, unsure if I would ever be okay again.

Mum wrung her hands, her face turning white.

Dad squeezed my hand; I felt him shaking. "We'll take you to the police. You need to report it."

"No! I mean... sorry, but the thought of more questions is too much for me. I want to lick my wounds in peace. Anyway, I didn't see who it was and I just want to forget about it. I don't need a doctor, either. I'll have a shower and something to eat."

I must have managed to convince them I was on the mend. They backed off and we watched a TV quiz before they got ready to leave.

Mum's parting words were, "You go and enjoy a long, hot shower. I'll call you later."

Stepping into the water, I turned the dial up. The sting of the water on my skin felt good. I remembered Karl being afraid of losing his pain and anger. I suddenly understood. This thought brought me to tears. I slowly sank to my knees as my skin turned redder. Had I been a fool to think I could help him? I didn't even know how to help myself.

Later, I ate some scrambled egg, which pleased Holly, but I could still feel her concern and suspicion.

"You don't need to worry; I'll survive." I remembered to turn the corners of my mouth up slightly.

"I would be less worried if you told me the truth. I thought we were best friends."

"We are! You've been good to me and I'm really grateful." Guilt pierced my chest. I wished it would kill me.

She wrinkled her brow and sat down at the table opposite me, "So explain why your toothpaste and toothbrush are missing if you were just going for a walk."

I pushed my plate away, putting my head in my hands. *Damn*! I hated lying to Holly, but I was certain she wouldn't believe the truth. She would suggest I needed a doctor. I would have no way of stopping her calling one in. The truth wasn't an option.

Raising my head from my arms I said, "Okay, there's this guy."

"I knew it!" she exclaimed. "Tell me who hurt you. I'll kill him!"

As her anger hit me, I groaned in desperation. It was an assault on my battered psyche. She meant well, and I loved her, but I couldn't cope with her feelings. I wasn't strong enough yet, and I didn't want to think about Karl, let alone talk about him. Ignoring my pain, I continued. "It's complicated, Holly. I don't want to lie to you, but I can't tell you everything."

"Why not?"

"Because he's done some really bad things in the past, and I can't tell anyone about him. I don't want you involved." This was stupid; her fear and intrigue was instant.

"What do you mean? You're living in my house. I'd say that makes me involved. Is he in trouble with the police?"

Shit. In all the time I had known Holly, this was the first time I had heard her raise her voice.

"No. The police don't even know about him and it has to stay that way." I frantically tried to find my next words. It was hard to think with my mind spinning in panic and my heart twisting with grief.

Her face was contorted with shock. "Oh my God, Emily, what have you got yourself into?"

"I wish I knew." I tried to keep my voice steady, wanting to calm her with no idea how. I babbled. "I met him at the Manor. He's related to Tom, but Tom told him to keep away from me because, well, because he didn't want me getting hurt. But I did meet him and I liked him. He made me laugh and it was exciting meeting him secretly. He had a spare key to the Manor and I met him there Boxing Day."

That was as close to the truth as I dared go. I hoped it would satisfy her. I closed my eyes, trying to will away the memory. My mind was cruel, playing me a picture of the stars, his arm around me, and his twinkling green eyes. A tear squeezed free from my lashes.

Holly's raised voice brought me back again. "And he attacked you? You need to tell the police!"

"No, he wouldn't hurt me." As I said it, I knew it was true.

She shook her head in confusion. "Why are you so upset then?"

"Another woman. She turned up while I was there and they were obviously lovers, or had been at least." My mind cruelly conjured up a picture of the two of them together, in bed. Bile rose in my throat again. I buried my face in my hands. "I don't want to talk about him anymore." "Okay, but you promise he didn't hurt you?"

"Yes," I muttered into my hands, "well, not physically." I didn't tell her it would have been preferable if it had been a physical wound he'd dealt me.

She took my plate and left me for a while. I could feel her worrying, and the gaze of her anxious eyes was never far from me.

Later, she asked calmly, "How did you end up falling for him? You're so sensitive to people's feelings. How could he have tricked you?"

"My sensitivities are a bit hit and miss."

She shrugged. "You always get it right with me. I can never hide anything from you."

I smiled at her. "True, but I've known you since we were three. We're like sisters. I think sometimes my own feelings get mixed up with other peoples' feelings. It's hard to tell which are mine and which are theirs. Maybe I just felt what I wanted to feel. Or maybe he did care. Just not enough to be faithful."

She nodded and squeezed my arm. "Just be careful, Okay." She waited for me to nod, then asked. "What are you going to do about work? Will you go back there?"

I shrugged. "I'm not sure." It was another question I wanted to avoid. If it had been an office block or a shop, it would have been much easier to walk away, however nice my employer was. Could I leave the manor? It had become such a part of my life, like a living, breathing thing.

Holly patted my hand and got up. "I'm going to the shop. Do you want anything?"

"How about the biggest bar of chocolate you can find?"

She chuckled. "You must be feeling better."

Once Holly had left, I sat wondering what to do. Slowly, a tiny fire started somewhere deep inside me. I still believed I was meant to be in the manor. I also remembered how I had felt, being with Karl.

Holly was right. I *was* sensitive to peoples' feelings. It might not be an exact science, but I should trust my instincts. He *did* feel something for me.

Was I really about to walk away and let Ana win? The thought of her poisonous lips kissing Karl fuelled the flames inside me. I prepared myself to fight the darkness.

The next day, Tom came to visit me. I still felt wretched, but I managed to hide the pieces of my torn up soul behind a calm façade. I decided the mugging story was the best one to stick with and tried to ignore Holly raising her eyebrows when I told him the lie. I felt more guilt, especially as he'd brought me an enormous bunch of yellow and red roses. I wondered if he knew that yellow stood for friendship and red for romantic love.

I told Tom I would be back at work within a few days. He was very understanding, which only served to make me feel even more ashamed.

I couldn't sleep that night; anxiety was like a knotted ball in my chest, and my head hurt with the constant battle going on inside it. I wanted to work; I wanted to go back to the manor; I wanted Tom as a friend, but was I ready to face Karl? *How the hell are you going to find out if he really loves you if you avoid him? You love him. He loves you. Fight for him!*

I decided he *was* worth fighting for. So was our love. But I was left with an agonising question. *Why didn't he stand up for me?*

My eyes snapped open. *What was that?* I felt something...or someone. With a racing heart, I flung back the covers and jumped from the bed. Hurrying to the window, I peered out. As my eyes searched the twilight below, a shape detached itself from the trees; the shape of a man; the shape of Karl. I couldn't see his face, but I knew it was him. He stood there for a few moments as if checking he had my attention and then moved towards Holly's car.

I couldn't see what he did exactly, but it looked like he was putting something on her car. Then he was gone. As I let out a breath, I realised I had stopped breathing. I wanted to hate him with every fibre of my body, but excitement had me running down the stairs. I got to the door and halted, my mind catching up with me. What if he was out there in the dark? Was I ready to face him?

In the end, it was sheer stubbornness that made me wait. I was not going to run out there like an infatuated idiot. Even if I was one.

Certain he was still out there, I crept back up to my room and crawled under the duvet to wait for the first light of dawn to drive him away.

The waiting was torture; excitement fizzed through my veins. Every tiny piece of my heart cried out to be in his arms again.

What has he left for me? A letter? A love letter? A goodbye letter? No! Please don't let it be over.

I wondered why he had picked her car when mine was parked right beside it. I guessed he probably thought I'd be more eager to retrieve it if I thought my friend might find it first.

With the sunlight bringing in the day, I heard Holly in the shower. I pulled on my robe, crept from my room and padded down the stairs, suddenly terrified there would be nothing to find.

Outside, heart fluttering, I headed for Holly's car. Tucked behind the windscreen wiper was a white envelope with the letter E on it. I picked it up and hurried back inside. As the door clicked shut behind me, I heard Holly coming down the stairs. I shoved the envelope in the pocket of my robe.

"What are you up to, Emily?" She glanced from me to the door. "Have you been outside?"

"Yes... I thought I heard someone in the front garden, but it must have been a cat or something." Another lie. Another nail of guilt hammered home.

I glanced at the stairs, desperate to escape my friend's innocent face, rush to my room and tear the envelope open. I clenched my fists against my screaming nerves and pasted a smile on my face.

She looked at me for a moment. "Well, now we're up, we may as well have a coffee." I felt her concern and wondered how bad I looked. Awful, probably, after no sleep. The fake smile probably made me look more manic than happy. I resigned myself to a coffee with her in the kitchen.

With mugs of coffee, we chatted across the kitchen table. Actually, she chatted about her work and I tried to make appropriate nods and smiles while my fingers clutched the letter in my pocket and my mind lurched between fear and hope, mostly fear. A small part of me wanted her to keep talking forever.

Eventually, she had to get ready for work, and I made it to my room. I sat on my bed, took the envelope out of my pocket and touched the elegant letter E, written in blue ink. I stared, my brain wondering if it would be better if I just threw it away. I couldn't do it; my heart took over and my hands tore the top from the envelope. Just a few lines:

> *Why do you still doubt me?*
> *At least let me talk to you*
> *The house needs you*
> *Tom needs you*
> *I need you*
>
> *K* xx

I read it until I could see it when I closed my eyes. *I need you*. It wasn't *I love you*, but it still made my spirits soar. Then my brain caught up and I crashed. What could he say that would make any difference? Maybe he didn't care about Ana, and maybe he did care about me, but he still stood there and let her make a fool of me. The ink started to run; a tear had fallen onto the kisses. It didn't seem like something he would normally do; put kisses on a letter. Was it an afterthought, to soften me up and make me go back? Or perhaps he really did want to show me he cared.

I wiped my eyes and put the letter in my bedside cabinet. Later that day, I rang Tom and told him I would be back to work the following Monday.

January...

This time, when I stood on the driveway and looked up at the house, I felt even more nervous than I did the first time I stood there. This time, it was about more than just a job. It was about friendship and love and destiny. I smiled as I walked up the frosty steps; I was home.

Tom made such a fuss of me that first day back, I felt like the lady of the house rather than the cleaner. I was too nervous to risk seeing Karl, even though it was my heart's truest desire. I asked Tom if I could help him with the horses. He was obviously delighted at my interest and said I was more than welcome. I don't pretend to know much about horses, but I do know that, like most animals, they give so much and yet ask for so little in return.

I understood Tom's love for them completely. They were uncomplicated and loyal. He showed me how to brush them down and I helped give them fresh hay and water. Their breath clouded the cold air as I smoothed their sleek necks.

My hands and feet were numb with cold as we walked back to the manor, and my hair had been whipped into a tangle by the wind, but my soul was warming.

Tom cleared his throat. "Would... would you like to come for a ride with me sometime?"

Looking up at him, I swallowed hard. The warmth of his feelings was a pleasant tonic, but I didn't want him to think I fancied him. I was afraid that saying no would offend him, and I did want to go riding. "I... would love to, but I'm not a good rider."

"Have you ridden at all?"

"Yes, but not for a while. I had lessons when I was younger, but I could never afford a horse of my own. I never learned how to care for one."

"They like you; I can tell. You have a natural way with them and have no fear. They can sense if someone fears them?" He stopped then and turned to face me. "I'm so glad you have come back to us."

"Us?" My heart did a jump. Did he know?

"Yes, me and the house. It's empty without you."

Relief flooded through me. "Nonsense!" I was a little embarrassed by his attention. "I'm only the cleaner, nothing more."

"Oh, but you are more, Emily, much more." He suddenly seemed flustered and turned a little pink in the cheeks. "What I mean is, you're a good friend."

I felt myself blush too, and the tingling feeling rising up my legs alarmed me. I had never felt this way about Tom. I stumbled for words. "Thank you, I'm glad you think so." I looked away, confused by the heat in my body.

We continued walking, and I glanced sideways at him, trying to make sense of my reactions. I was not attracted to him; I knew I wasn't. So the feelings must be his. I groaned inside. Agreeing to go riding would encourage him further.

I had to back off before his feelings deepened. My life was a big enough mess already. Yet, how much simpler life would be if I could just love dear Tom.

On Tuesday, I worked briskly, dusting and polishing everything in sight, trying to block out both men. It seemed the faster I worked, the faster my brain spun tangled thoughts of Karl and Tom, mostly Karl.

By the time Tom went to feed the horses, I was so tired I collapsed in a chair in the conservatory to take my break. I deliberately chose this space because it was light. The winter sun had managed to break free from its chains and shine amongst the clouds for a while. I wasn't sure if I was ready to face Karl.

As I basked in the warmth, my eyes became heavy and I allowed them to rest. A sound, a rustling noise. My eyes snapped open. *Karl?* I got up and walked towards the adjoining music room. The green velvet curtains were hooked back and the vertical blinds were only partially closed, allowing the sunlight to run in streaks across the parquet floor and over the grand piano.

Glancing into the shadowed corner of the room, I saw nothing, but as I stepped nearer to the piano, I noticed a rectangular parcel, wrapped in red Christmas paper, on the floor.

I stared at the parcel for a moment, then went over and picked it up; it was heavier than I expected and solid. I read the label.

This was meant to be your Christmas present

K xx

My heart danced as I peered back to the shadows. This time, I noticed one of the wooden wall panels didn't line up with the rest. Gripping the parcel tightly in one arm, I moved quickly to the panel and pushed my fingers into a small crack at one side. The wood slid to the right, revealing a gap slightly wider than my body.

"Karl. Are you there?"

I squinted into the darkness, then gave up and retreated to an armchair. Carefully, I stripped the paper from my present. Inside was a book. Not just any book. I ran my finger over the title – Wuthering Heights.

"I'm afraid I cheated."

My gaze shot from the book towards the gap in the wall. He emerged from the shadows and gave me a lopsided smile.

"I didn't buy you a present; it was already mine to give."

My heart danced, but I composed myself "You couldn't have bought me anything better. But you can't buy *me*." I stood and walked to the piano. Placing the book on top, I met his gaze. "All the gifts in the world could never make up for the humiliation you caused me. It won't happen again."

I took a step towards the conservatory, but he was too quick for me. He seemed to fly from the shadows and catch hold of my arm, but in doing so the sun found the skin of his hand. I heard a hiss, smelt burning flesh, and felt a sharp pain. As I turned he retreated to the shadows, hiding his hand from view. Concern propelled my feet towards him.

"You're being unfair," he whispered, his hand behind his back, his voice filled with pain.

I felt it too, more than just physical. I couldn't leave him.

"I had no idea Ana would arrive when she did. I completely forgot..."

"You forgot it was your usual arrangement! You also forgot to tell me she was your lover." The words burst out of me like a wild animal screeching in agony. I took a few breaths and managed to regain control. "So. Explain. If you can."

His eyes showed pain. "I hadn't seen her for months, certainly not since I met you in the garden that time. Meeting you pushed her right out of the picture. How can you be angry at that?

Was this true? Did it make a difference? Why the hell couldn't I be strong and simply walk away from this crazy, secret relationship with a jealous, two-timing vampire? I found myself moving closer, wanting his reassurance. "You still should have told me about her."

"Really? Would you have me tell you about all my past lovers? Only we could be here quite a while."

It was like a slap to my face. "Bastard!" My hand shot out to strike him, but he caught it with his good hand.

"I'm so sorry, Emily. I shouldn't have said that."

I tried to pull away, but he held my hand to his chest.

"You know what I feel, Emily, so feel it. You must know how lost I am without you, how wretched my existence is."

I knew, but it wasn't enough. "Why did you let her make fun of me?"

"Because she has a temper; I was afraid she would harm you."

Alarm ran through me. "Couldn't you have protected me?"

"Of course, but I didn't want to take any chances. It's best if she thinks you're not important to me. I should have realised that you would think the same. I'm sorry. I acted badly."

I tried to calm my breathing. "What did you tell her? Are you sure I'm not in danger?"

He nodded "I told her I was into humans at the moment. She wasn't happy, but she accepted it and left."

He still had hold of my hand and he was stroking it gently. I glanced down at the hand he had burnt and my mouth dropped open. I could see the skin healing. Red, blistered flesh was turning into smooth pale skin. His physical pain had faded, overridden by emotional pain. *It's magic. You're magic. But I haven't finished being angry with you.*

I looked into his eyes. "How can I ever trust you?"

"I have never lied to you, Emily. For God's sake, give me a chance. Please?" He gripped my shoulders. "Do you think this is easy for me? I've never felt like this for a woman before. Please don't expect me to know what to say and do all the time. I don't, and maybe I never will, but I can't bear to see you so sad and angry with me. I know I'm a better man since I met you. Please don't abandon me now."

His longing swam from his heart into mine, and my anger melted. He released my shoulders and I felt the loss of connection in my chest. "It's up to you now. I promise I won't keep chasing you if you don't want me, but I hope you do."

My inner battle intensified. I loved him, and I was angry because it made me vulnerable. I glanced toward the conservatory. The sunlight was seeping through the doorway. Should I walk towards it and away from Karl?

"I didn't ask to fall in love with a vampire." The words came out thoughtlessly. I avoided his gaze as we both realised what I'd said.

"You said love."

I kept my face turned away, not wanting to look at him.

"Look at me." He reached out with one hand and pushed my chin up.

Slowly, I raised my eyes to his.

"You said love. Did you mean it?" His gaze pinned me to the spot.

Fear gripped my heart. All my pride and dignity had been laid out before him. He could crush it at will now, and there was nothing I could do. *I can feel his love. Can't I? What if I'm wrong? Maybe it's just my own love for him I feel? No. This is real. It has to be.* I held my breath, ready to run away or jump. It was up to him now.

"Don't be afraid, Emily. I may have had sex with other women, but I've never made love to one. I hear there is a difference. I want to find out."

My breath came out in a rush. "You would need to be in love to find out. Are you capable?" Could I dare to believe it? My love welled up inside me, but so did my fear. My breaths came short and sharp, my body tensed, waiting for him to reply.

"Why don't you tell me?" He pulled my hands against his chest and pressed them to him. He didn't hold back his feelings from me, and the force of them made my legs weak. I collapsed into his arms as his love and desire flooded through me in waves.

I knew his anger and pain simmered underneath, but the fact that his love for me had conquered over them was nothing short of a miracle. I slid my hands up his chest and around his neck, standing on tiptoe to kiss him. He returned my kiss with passion.

We broke apart suddenly at the sound of the lawn mower starting outside. We both looked toward the window, startled.

"I'm sure Ned can't see in through those blinds," Karl said.

I nodded, "But we should be careful."

He pulled me into the gap between the wooden panels.

I peered into the gloom. "What is this? A secret passageway?" I asked.

"Yes. It allowed the servants to move around without getting in the family's way. Now we can move around without Tom knowing."

His soft chuckle in my ear sent a tingle down my spine.

"Will you come back later?" he murmured, kissing my neck.

I groaned. "How can I? I can't just knock on the door and ask for you, can I?" I frowned in frustration. Nothing would ever be simple. For a moment I froze: I was mortal and would grow old while he remained young! I pushed the horror away. All that mattered was right then and being with him.

He too had frozen. He blinked and shook his head. "No! Tom must never know about us; he'll be convinced I'm going to kill you. He's never had the nerve to stand up for himself, but he would for your sake." He sneered. "Good old Tom. Wouldn't *he* like to get you into bed!"

"Karl! You should be nicer to him. He works hard for the business and has to do many chores because you don't want more servants. I'd be sorry to lose him as a friend."

"I'm civil to him. Well, most of the time. He needs to get married and produce a son, but he seems to be more interested in moping around after you at the moment." He was teasing me; he seemed too happy to be annoyed.

"What nonsense!" I slapped his arm in play, then snuggled back into him. My head against his beating heart.

"I'm not a fool, Emily, and you must know how he feels. I know I can trust you, but he needs to meet someone else. Couldn't you tell him you have a boyfriend?"

"I suppose so, but I don't want to tell more lies."

"So, tell him he's tall dark and handsome," he joked. His lips were close to my ear, and his breath sent a shiver down my spine. Then he turned me to face him and kissed my forehead. "Park in the lane behind St Peter's church at eight tonight. I will get you in unnoticed."

I was still a little unsure after the last time, though I didn't bother trying to kid myself I wasn't going to turn up. I smiled up at him. "I'll be there."

He kissed me again. Then released me.

"Good, and I have your bag, so you won't need to bring anything."

"Okay, I'll go and put that book in my car before Tom comes back. Thanks again, I wasn't expecting you to give me anything." I was reluctant to go but had to get on with my work.

He was still grinning. "I wanted you to have it. You can do me a favour in return if you like." He had a glint in his eye.

Eyebrows raised, I asked, "And what would that be?"

"You could wear that red dress again."

I laughed and blew him a kiss as I left him in the shadows of the secret passage. I picked up the book and made my way out through the conservatory.

When I got to the car, I sat in the front seat and opened it. Inside was a note. He had written:

All my love, **K** *xx*

I held it to my heart and sighed a happy sigh.

K7

"See you later, Holly," I called. Grabbing my jacket, I walked quickly to the door, hoping to escape her scrutiny.

"Where are you going?"

I turned to find her, eyebrows raised and arms crossed, behind me. "Oh. Um..." I didn't want to tell her. I hated making her worry, but it was my life. I'd tried safe and been bored beyond reason.

"You're going to see him, aren't you?"

She knows. Damn.

"Emily!"

I sighed. "Give me a break, Holly. You're just as bad."

"What! When have you had to peel me off the floor broken hearted?"

"Okay, not quite that bad," I conceded, "but didn't your last boyfriend run up your credit card bill and nearly bankrupt you?"

She shrugged. "I guess we're both crap at picking men." With that, she resigned herself to my foolishness.

It had been a very long time since adrenaline had rushed through my veins so furiously, and I felt alive, *really* alive. I practically skipped to the car and grinned all the way to the manor.

Cutting the engine of my battered Fiesta, I reluctantly switched off the headlights, swallowed hard to control my anxiety, and stepped out into the surrounding darkness. I felt Karl's presence straight away, and when he whispered my name I realised it wasn't just *my* relief I felt, but his too.

He slipped his arms around my waist. "I was worried you wouldn't come," he murmured softly in my ear.

I chuckled, pleased he had shown me his vulnerable side. "It's unlike you to be unsure of yourself," I teased.

"You have a knack of unsettling me." His smile was warm as he gazed at me.

"Well, I'm here. Are you just going to stand there, or are you going to take me inside before I freeze?" I was amazed how confident I sounded; my insides were quivering.

As soon as I said it, I was up in his arms, and the world was passing me by at speed. I clung to his neck; laughing in his ear as he ran and leapt over the six-foot fence surrounding the Manor. He put me down beside the entrance to the passageway in the woods.

Grinning, he asked, "Can you manage the ladder in that dress?"

Grinning back at him, I replied, "I think so. Put it this way, I'm not taking it off to climb down there, so I'll have to."

It was warm in his rooms under the Manor. Electric heaters breathed out hot air and the lighting was low. Warmth filled my heart.

"Wine?" He held out a large glass of red wine, which I gratefully accepted. He sprawled out on the black velvet sofa and beckoned me to join him.

I sat next to him, aware of every place his body connected with mine. I felt him watching me as I drank the wine a little too quickly.

"Is the thought of sleeping with me frightening?" His hand stroked the back of my neck, sending shivers down my spine. I felt a tinge of concern on the edge of his desire.

"What? Oh. No. Well, not you in particular. Not that there's anyone else... I mean..." My face coloured as I fumbled for the right words to say. I was afraid of being compared to Ana and afraid I might plant the idea of her in his head if it wasn't there already. "It's been a while, that's all," I said, truthfully.

He took my hand gently in his. "You do know I wouldn't harm you, don't you?"

I nodded, reaching out with my free hand and touching his face. He leant forward, brushing his soft cool lips against mine. Shuddering with pleasure, I pulled his face towards me. He kissed me again, more deeply this time. His tongue flicked against mine, causing a jolt of sexual energy, so strong I arched my back and gripped his hair in my fist. Scooping me up in his arms, he carried me into his bedroom.

He gently laid me on his oak, four-poster bed. As the full power of his love, lust and passion hit me, my anxiety melted away. We struggled free of our clothes, our lips only parting for a few moments, and I almost slid off the bed. He pulled me back to him, laughing.

I giggled into his chest as heat fizzed through my body.

His lips left a trail of kisses from my breasts to my navel, then from my ankles to the tops of my thighs, until I moaned in anticipation. My chest rose and fell with deep heavy breaths as his tongue followed the same trail down my body to my naval, then further exploring the most intimate part of me, until I trembled and writhed under him. I cried out his name and pulled him into me, letting him fill me completely; our bodies and feelings combined as if we were one. I clung to him as he shuddered and murmured my name against my ear.

When he rolled from me, breathing heavily, he folded me in his arms. He held me tightly as if I were a lifeboat protecting him from a sea of emotions he couldn't control. He whispered in my ear, "I love you, Emily."

"I love you too," I replied softly, with a heart so full of joy I could have wept. "So... is making love different? Do you have the answer you wanted?"

He kissed my forehead, then took my hand, pressing it to his chest. "I don't think I have the words to explain how I feel."

I looked into his eyes and found myself swimming in an emerald sea of emotions. It was deep, but so beautiful, that I wanted to drown. I fell asleep with him stroking my hair. I dreamt I was floating, looking up at the stars.

I woke up in total darkness, smiling at the memory of the night before. Stretching out my hand, I found myself alone. My eyes snapped open. Heart pounding, I sat bolt upright in bed. *God, surely he hasn't gone out and left me here alone!* Fear gripped my chest.

"Emily, are you okay?" His voice came out of the darkness from the corner of the room.

"You're still here! I couldn't see you." My heart slowed its pace as relief flooded through me.

"Sorry, I thought the light would wake you. I needed to feed."

An image of him drinking blood pierced my brain, sending a shudder through my body. I heard him move across the room before the light came on. As my eyes adjusted, he sat on the bed beside me. In his hand was an empty, see-through plastic bag; traces of deep red liquid remained in the creases.

For the rest of the night, sleep eluded me

February...

I was happy in a way you can only be when you take nothing for granted. I knew I could lose him at any minute. I knew he was dangerous. But my life had meaning, and I owed it to him. I didn't expect a happy ending; how could I? I was human: he wasn't, I loved the sun: he didn't, I was getting older: he wasn't – the list of impossibilities went on, yet I loved him to distraction.

We spent many nights in his room together and walked in the woods under the stars. During the day, when Tom wasn't around, he read to me or played the piano. We would talk and laugh. Sometimes he helped me with my work, which always amused me because he clearly hadn't a clue what he was doing. Still, I loved him for trying. I was often reminded of his darker side; his jealousy, his volatile nature. But I always forgave him. I knew he was angry because he couldn't cope with the strength of his own feelings.

Sometimes, when he walks towards me, eyes flashing, I wonder, does he want to kill me or kiss me? I'm not entirely sure. He's tormented by feelings of pain and confusion; he's tormented more by love. I know because I feel it too. But which does he want to do most, kill me or kiss me? Do I mind either way? I would rather die at his hands than live without him.

Picking up a magazine on Karl's sofa one day, I was surprised to see it was a motorbike magazine.

"I didn't know you like motorbikes," I called, looking over my shoulder to where he was studying the computer screen.

He finished an email and joined me on the sofa. "I was going to tell you about that. Sorry, I was busy when you got here; a business deal."

I raised my eyebrows. "Oh?"

He shook his head dismissively. "You wouldn't find it interesting." He took the magazine from me and leafed through it. "This on the other hand." Grinning like a child, he showed me a picture of a black sporty-looking bike. "The roads have been too icy to ride, but it's milder now. Benedikte wrote off my last bike. This beauty arrives tomorrow."

His excitement was infectious. I grinned back. "Wow!"

"You like it?" he asked.

"I don't know much about bikes," I confessed. "But it looks like fun."

"I'm glad you think so." His grin widened further. "I've got a spare helmet and jacket for you, so we'll go for a spin tomorrow night."

He misunderstood my panicked face. "Don't worry. I won't go too fast with you on the back."

"It's not that. Karl, you know I go out with Holly Wednesday nights. I'll go for a ride with you Thursday."

He scowled, his anger burning my chest. "Tell her you're busy."

I recoiled, surprised by the venom in his voice. "We've already arranged to meet the others now. Why can't it wait until Thursday?"

"Because the bike arrives tomorrow. By others, you mean who exactly?"

"Friends, just friends."

"Including your male friends?"

I frowned. How did he know a couple of our friends were men? I deliberately hadn't said so. "Have you been following me?" I gritted my teeth, trying to keep my anger from flaring.

His eyes shifted sideways. "I just noticed you all leaving the pub one night. One of them walked you home."

He's been watching me, *damn him*! My fury bubbled in my chest. "Then you'll have noticed he said goodbye and left at the doorstep! That was Lee, for God's sake. He's had a thing for Holly for ages."

Karl's anger cracked with uncertainty; he looked down at his hands.

I wasn't prepared to leave it there. "I have no idea what you get up to when I'm not around, and I'm not sure I want to." He looked up and went to speak. I held my hand up to silence him. With eyebrows raised, he let me continue. "I don't keep questioning you about women. I don't even ask you to stay away from Ana."

"I told you it's over with her. Besides, staying away from her would be difficult; she's Benedikte's sister." He looked at me beseechingly, but hot molten energy boiled over inside me.

"Difficult!" I yelled, jumping up from the sofa. "Don't you think cutting out all my friends would be *difficult* for me?" He opened his mouth to protest, but I didn't give him a chance. "No," I shouted, pacing the room. "You never think about how difficult this relationship is for me! What do you want? Me with no friends, pathetically waiting for you to show up?" I kicked the table in frustration, sending a glass of wine flying.

The sound of glass shattering and the sight of the red stain spreading on the beige carpet left me stunned at my own outburst. I turned to Karl, who was sitting open mouthed and wide eyed.

"Emily, calm down. You're right, I didn't think. I'm not used to having to." Standing, he reached out for my hand.

My eyes filled with tears. I'd meant every word, but I didn't want a fight. "You're going to have to learn if you want to be with me, Karl. I don't want to lose my friends."

Pulling me to him, he whispered, "And I don't want to lose you."

"You won't." I looked into his emerald eyes and sighed. "I'd better clean up that mess. Pulling away, I studied the carpet. "I'll pick up the glass first. Do you have a brush down here?" As I spoke, I walked to a door I assumed was a cupboard and put my hand out to open it.

He was there before me, blocking my way. "Leave it. I'll sort it out later."

Surprised by the abruptness of his reaction and the sudden wave of anxiety in his emotions, I stopped. "But the wine will stain."

"Get a cloth from the kitchen; I'll pick up the glass." His voice was curt, but when my eyes filled with tears again, he softened. "I just don't want you cutting yourself, and there's nothing but spare linen in there."

We mopped up the wine together on our hands and knees, giggling and shoving each other. When I was finally satisfied the carpet was clean, I allowed his caresses to excite me.

It was Thursday evening; I squealed with delight as I clung to Karl. Streetlights flashed by, followed by the darkness of the countryside. All my worries blew away in the cold night air. The engine throbbed between my thighs, sending heat through every vein in my body. Stopping at a remote country Inn, he flipped up his visor and said, "Let's go in for a drink."

"Ooh, like a proper date?" I giggled, removing my helmet and getting off the bike.

He laughed, joining me and linking my arm through his. It was good to act like an ordinary couple, talking and laughing at the bar. Bourbon warmed my insides while the open fire warmed my skin.

By morning, my unrest had returned. In the shower, I kept thinking about the cupboard. Why was he so uptight about it? Then I fell into wondering if he was grabbing the chance to feed while I was out of the way. I pushed the image of the blood bag away and switched off the water. Think positive; the spring is up ahead. But even that turned into a negative. I stepped out of the shower and padded into the bedroom wrapping a towel around my body.

"Karl...how will we manage when the nights get shorter?"

He lounged on the bed, wearing tight black boxer shorts. "It would be much easier if you lived in the house."

I turned to him as I combed my hair. "There's nothing I would like more, but Tom would be suspicious."

"Not if he thought it was his idea." He swung his legs over the side of the bed and looked at me earnestly.

"You already get angry because you think Tom has feelings for me." I hunted in my bag for my clean clothes as I spoke.

"We both know he has feelings for you." His voice was serious, but not harsh. "I hate it when you agree to go riding with him, even though I trust you."

"There you go. Even if you accept he's my friend, it's begrudging. How can I live in the same house as him? Wouldn't it be leading him on? And why would he come up with the idea? You said he wants to keep me away from you, and he doesn't like me being on the premises after dark."

"I'm sure I could convince him I'm not interested in a lowly cleaner." He grinned and hid behind a pillow as I threw my deodorant can at him.

"Bloody cheek! This lowly cleaner is the best thing that happened to you."

He darted behind me and grabbed my towel away. "I can't argue with that."

"Stop it. Can't you ever be serious?" I tried to sound cross, but he was grinning, his green eyes twinkling, and I struggled not to laugh.

"Leave it to me. I'll think of something, I promise." He pulled me against him, but for once I resisted his kisses.

"We need to leave soon, and I'm not being carried out of here naked, so please let me dress."

"Okay, if I must," he said with a smile as he went off to shower.

I finished dressing and wandered into the living room to wait. My eyes rested on the cupboard door. Was it really a linen cupboard? I was drawn toward it like a magnet. My fingers hovered over the handle. I could hear the shower still running as I turned the knob; the door wouldn't budge. I stepped back. Why would anyone keep their linen cupboard locked?

On Saturday night, Holly and I were in *The Flying Pig* as usual, and it was packed with people. It was a live music night; the band, Primeval Years, was doing sound checks. I hadn't heard of them, but I liked live music and looked forward to it.

The atmosphere was charged as the electric guitar cried out the first notes of *Sweet Child of Mine* by Guns and Roses. Holly grabbed my hand and we pushed our way to the dance floor. We danced through several rock songs, bumping against other swaying bodies. Then we made our way to the bar and ordered our drinks.

Holly leant over and shouted in my ear. "He's hot!"

My gaze followed her finger to the band. "Which one?"

"The lead singer. Look at those abs."

As she spoke, the man in question turned his gaze on her.

I grabbed her hand and shouted back to her. "Holly. Stop pointing and gawping. Do you have to be so obvious?"

She laughed and threw back some of her vodka and coke.

At the end of the set, the lead singer fixed his mike to the stand and jostled towards us through the people. Reaching the bar, he stood the other side of Holly, raised his hand to the bartender and ordered a lager.

Holly took another gulp of drink and turned to him. They struck up a conversation and I wandered off to search for our friend, Lee. I found him gloomily nursing a beer in the corner. "Hey, Lee, what's up?" I fell into a seat next to him.

He looked up with a half-hearted grin. "Hi, Ems. Nothing's up."

I raised my eyebrows and waited.

He grimaced. "Well, nothing except I'm not as interesting as Mr Rock Star." He glanced over to the bar where Holly was still deep in conversation with her muscle-bound companion. With his short-cropped hair, he reminded me of an action man. I watched as Holly giggled like a schoolgirl.

I sighed. "Sorry, Lee, but you know she likes the bad boys. You're much too nice."

"Typical." He rolled his eyes and sighed. "Funny, women always moan about men not treating them right, but if you respect them, they're turned off because you're boring Mister Nice."

"I know; life's not fair, is it?" I looked up to see Holly heading in our direction, followed by the singer. "Sorry Lee, but they're heading this way."

He groaned but plastered a smile on his face. Whatever he thought, I knew he would never say anything to embarrass her.

When they got to our table, Holly introduced her companion as Daniel Stone.

He smiled and held out his hand "Hi, nice to meet you."

As he spoke, the hairs on the back of my neck stood on end. I held my breath as his eyes lingered on Holly. I shuddered. He looked normal enough. Why were my senses telling me to run?

"Can I buy you guys a drink?" he asked.

No! I wanted to scream, but the only feelings I could pick up on were positive. I glanced at Lee, guessing he would rather snog a porcupine than join this man for a drink.

"Thanks," Lee jumped in, "but I was just about to get us one." He hopped up and disappeared to the bar, leaving Daniel with raised eyebrows.

Holly turned her smile into a short laugh. "He's a bit shy,"

"I should get back to the stage," Daniel said, touching Holly's arm. "I'll see you later."

He walked away, and the band soon started their next set.

Holly landed in the chair next to me. "He's sooo fit," she gushed, "and he's asked me to go out for a drink with him. This is their last gig for a while, but he's going to hang around. He's staying in a room upstairs."

"Slow down! You don't even know him. I seem to remember you telling me to be careful the other day."

She laughed. "I didn't say *I* was staying up there with him. Besides, I seem to remember you ignoring me."

I smiled, trying to shake my concerns. Holly was so excited, and who was I to judge?

At the end of the set, I made my way to the ladies. I jostled my way back towards the bar. In the crush, I managed to come face-to-face with Daniel.

His blue eyes met mine; he grinned. "Hi, Emily."

"Oh...Hi." Had the temperature dropped suddenly? Why was I shivering?

"Holly told me you've been friends since nursery school. That's pretty cool."

I nodded, the thought warming me a little. "She's an amazing girl."

"Talking about me, I hope." Holly's happy face peered around his arm.

"Of course." He said with a wide smile. "Look, I need to go and help the guys pack the equipment away. Don't go anywhere without saying goodbye." He gave me a sideways glance as he walked away. Something cold crawled through my belly.

Lee appeared at my elbow. He always walked us home from the pub. "Ready when you are, girls."

"Wait," said Holly, "I promised to say goodbye to Daniel." She skipped over to the band, who were busy unplugging wires and moving speakers.

Lee looked at me with a pained expression. I shrugged and hoped he would soon find someone else to moon after.

Holly soon returned with a grin covering her entire face. "Daniel's coming with us. He says he could do with some fresh air."

I wanted to say, no way, but I was scared Holly would simply go off with him alone. I glanced at Lee and guessed he feared the same.

He sighed. "Well, okay. But we all stick together, and he goes when we get to your place. You've just met him... and what with Emily's recent ordeal."

I frowned. *What recent ordeal?* Then I remembered my mugging story. Daniel sauntered over, and we all left together. The night was warm, and the streetlights lit our way. Holly and Daniel walked behind, Holly's laughter ringing out through the streets. We came to a stop by the door. *Don't invite him in, please.* The thought of it freaked me out.

"Thanks, Daniel," Holly gushed.

"Thanks, Lee," I added.

Holly glanced at Lee, then went back to gazing at Daniel.

He returned her gaze. "Maybe we could meet up tomorrow. I'll give you my number, then you can ring me if you're interested."

Holly pulled out her phone and fed his number in.

Daniel glanced at me and Lee. "I'll say goodnight. Gotta get back and help load the van." With a final smile for Holly, he turned and strolled back down the road.

Lee said bye and headed the other way. Holly and I went inside, and I gratefully closed the door.

That night I lay in bed. Daniel Stone rolled around in my head until my brain felt like pulp. I wished I could call Karl, but with no reception in his quarters, it was pointless. For some reason, he didn't even own a mobile. I couldn't call the landline because Tom would answer. The isolation from Karl hadn't bothered me before; I liked the notes he left me to find, but that night, I badly needed to talk to him, and sleep took a long time coming.

All the next day, I watched the clock, waiting for the evening, so I could talk with Karl. My anxiety rocketed when Holly called Daniel to arrange a meeting, but to my surprise, she took my advice for once and met him for lunch in the pub. She came back full of how he was a perfect gentleman. It left me wondering if I had imagined my unease, but I couldn't shake the feeling.

Finally, it was time to meet Karl. I gathered my coat and was out the door in a flash.

Karl welcomed me into his quarters. The fire was glowing and softly lit the room. We settled cosily together on the sofa, and I immediately launched into my concerns. "Last night, the singer in the band asked Holly out."

Karl's nestled in closer and planted kisses on my cheek and ear and hair. "He was pleasant enough, but I think he was hiding something. I got a bad feeling from him, but I'm not sure why."

He stopped the kissing and picked up the TV remote. "I'm sure Holly's old enough to choose her own boyfriends. I don't see why I should care." He flicked through the channels. "What do you want to watch? Or do you want to come to bed?" He slid his hand up my thigh.

I stopped it with my own and faced him. "Karl, please listen. I'm worried about her. Something isn't right."

He sighed and switched the TV off. "You probably picked up that his intentions weren't particularly honourable. He'd just got off stage and pulled a girl. What do you expect for goodness sake?"

"It isn't her honour I'm concerned about. If she wants to get off with some loser, that's her affair, but what if he's dangerous?"

"Did you pick up on any anger or malice?"

"Not really. If anything, he seemed pleased, too pleased."

He laughed. "You're worried because he seemed pleased?

I pushed his hand away and stood up. "Yes, you're right. How stupid of me to worry. I'm concerned he may be dangerous and here I am sleeping with a vampire. What could I possibly know about dangerous men?" I stomped away and went to leave his rooms, only to find him blocking my way.

His eyes had narrowed dangerously, their colour deepening. His voice was measured and cool. "Don't have a go at me; I haven't done anything to hurt your friend. And more to the point, how many times were you asked out last night?"

It's about time he started to trust me. And realise he doesn't own me. Foolishly, I goaded him further. "I don't remember; I had quite a lot to drink."

His rage hit me like a physical punch; I stumbled back, clutching my chest; his face softened as his anger dissolved.

I quickly relented, wondering if one day I would push him too far. *Idiot! Why do you do that?* But even through my fear, I felt the tingle of excitement that danger always brings.

"I'm sorry, Karl; you know you can trust me. I didn't really get drunk." I sat in the chair, looking up at him, my heart hammering against my ribs. "I'm loyal to people I care about, that's why I'm so worried for Holly."

He sighed. "Okay, what was this man's name?"

"Daniel Stone. He's well built, like military."

He thought for a moment, "No, the name doesn't mean anything to me, but I could find out about him if you want."

"Yes please, but can you just let me know? I don't want you to do anything."

"No, of course not." He grinned, not a pleasant grin.

"I mean it, Karl!"

He held up his palms. "Okay, okay. You're wish is my command. What was the band called?"

"Primeval Years."

"Mmm, strange name."

"Most bands have strange names, especially rock bands."

He picked up a pen and wrote the name down at the edge of his newspaper. I watched, fascinated, as he played with the letters for a while. Finally, he turned the paper around and showed me the anagram he had written;

Vampire slayer

My jaw dropped as I looked at him, wide-eyed.

"What does it mean?"

"Maybe nothing; just a coincidence. Or, maybe we have a problem."

K8

I slumped back onto Karl's sofa, turning the anagram over in my mind. "It must be a coincidence," I said hopefully.

He perched beside me; brow furrowed. "Could be he wanted to get a connection to me, which would explain why you picked up odd vibes from him."

I could sense his unease. "Do you think all the band members could be vampire hunters?"

"Possibly, but there's no way of knowing. It's a bit daft, though. Why would they make their name so obvious? They can't be that good at their job."

"The only thing obvious to me is the way he latched onto Holly so readily. Perhaps they're trying to goad you. It could be a trap. What I don't get, is how he even knows about you, and how would he know that we're connected?" I ran my fingers through my hair. It was all too confusing.

He stood and paced the room, then looked at me sharply. "What did you tell Holly about me?"

"Nothing much. I told her I was seeing a relative of Tom's in secret. Obviously, I didn't tell her what you are, or your name. Anyway, she hadn't even met him before, so someone else must have talked to him."

We looked at each other and both said, "Ana!"

I shook my head, "It doesn't make sense. Why would a vampire help a vampire hunter?"

He thumped the wall with his hand. "Jealousy. She didn't take kindly to me sending her away." Walking to the chair, he crouched in front of me and took my hand, kissing it tenderly. I'm sorry, I've put you in danger. Maybe you should stay away from me for a while."

His touch made my heart race. The thought of staying away from him, made my chest hurt. "Is he likely to harm me?

Surely, he'll just try and get information from me, or follow me."

He squeezed my hand against his beating heart. "Or, he may harm you to get to me."

"Only if he thinks you care enough about me to stop him."

He thought for a minute, "Here's what we'll do…"

Holly paced up and down the living room, wringing her hands. She was waiting for Daniel to turn up. They had spent Sunday afternoon together and she seemed quite giddy with the thought of him. It made me sick.

He'd told her he ran a private-detective agency. Being in a band allowed him to move around without any questions being asked.

I longed to share my suspicions with Holly, but it was impossible to explain the anagram and that I was terrified her boyfriend could be a vampire slayer trying to kill my vampire!

I picked up a book and pretended to read, but my mind raced. If I told her, she'd think I'd gone mad. And if she believed me, she's want to protect me from Karl. She would see Daniel as a hero and me as a fool.

I looked up and saw Holly preening her auburn curls in the mirror. My stomach churning, knowing I was deceiving her, I forced a cheerful voice, "You look great; stop worrying."

She turned and grinned, her excitement meeting me in waves. I swallowed hard, trying to remove my heart from my throat. I knew he was using her, and I knew I had to find a way to protect both her and Karl. I truly believed I was doing the right thing. At the time.

I switched on the TV and turned to meet with Holly's raised eyebrows.

"Aren't you going out tonight?" she asked.

I shook my head and looked away as if I didn't want to talk. Daniel's car pulled up outside.

Holly's concern danced through me.

When I turned to her, the tears in my eyes were real.

"You go out and have fun. I'll be okay."

The doorbell rang and she hesitated, studying my face.

"He's hurt you again hasn't he?"

"I'll be fine, honestly. I let myself be made a fool of. It won't happen again. We're through." I gave a weak smile as the doorbell went again.

She frowned and slightly shook her head. "You never even told me his name."

I glanced towards the door and managed a grin. "He won't wait forever, and I'm missing my TV programme. Go! I'm fine."

With her brown eyes sparkling, she blew me a kiss and left.

I wondered how much she would tell Daniel about me. Would she tell him she was concerned about my *ex-boyfriend*? Was Daniel really using her to find out about me, or rather Karl? What would he do when he found out she didn't have much to tell? I paced up and down the living room. *As long as he's nice to her.*

Eventually, I tired of pacing and sat down to watch the film, *Marley and Me*. It wasn't a sensible move. If there is one thing guaranteed to make me cry, it's sad animal films. I was wiping my eyes with a tissue when I heard the front door open. I turned to see Holly, followed by Daniel.

"You're back early." I was surprised, considering how excited she was about going out. I got up, ready to make myself scarce.

"Daniel thought we should check you're okay. Hey...you've been crying."

"Oh, only over a soppy film. I'm fine. I'll get out of your way." *Is that annoyance I detect, Holly? Not that I'm surprised*

106

if your date was ruined because of me. Hang on... I looked at Daniel. "How come you thought you needed to check on me?" I glanced at Holly, who looked sheepish, then back to him.

He smiled. "You're right. She did mention something about you having boyfriend trouble. The pub was overcrowded, and we thought you could use a bit of company."

I hesitated, looking at Holly. Normally, I would have been annoyed to know she was talking about my private life to a man she hardly knew, but I guessed Daniel had wormed things out of her.

"I hope we're not intruding," he continued. "If you'd like me to leave..."

I still hovered, unsure what to do. Him coming back like this was a surprise, but maybe I could use it as a chance to get information. *Play it cool.*

I looked at my friend. "I'm sure Daniel doesn't want to listen to my problems." I was actually sure he did because I could feel his interest, as if it were a physical thing.

Daniel's smiled warmly. "Didn't you mention a drink, Holly? Perhaps Emily would like one too?"

I nodded and she dashed off to the kitchen.

Daniel settled into a chair. "So, boyfriend trouble." His smile was fake; so was the one I returned.

I shrugged and sat on the sofa. "Not anymore. I don't want to see him again."

"She's very secretive about him," Holly called from the kitchen.

Daniel appeared relaxed, but I knew his brain was in overdrive.

I rolled my eyes. "I'm not being secretive; I don't know anything! We met in secret. I don't know where he lives. I don't even know if the name he gave me is real."

Daniel's eyebrows went up. "You're kidding. What name did he give you?"

"Karl Ashton," I told him as planned. "But I've never heard Tom mention him, which is weird if he let him stay in his house. To be honest, the whole situation is weird. I wonder if he's married."

I heard Holly tut at this, and I turned to take the wine she had poured me.

"I think his marital status could be the least of her worries," Daniel said in a concerned tone.

Holly sat next to me on the sofa and patted my knee. "Thank God you're through with him. You can do sooo much better. Look at me."

I gave a weak smile as she looked from me to Daniel.

Daniel winked at Holly, then turned his attention back to me. "Let us know if you get any more aggro from him. I've got plenty of contacts in the force."

"Thanks."

"No problem." He leant across to Holly and squeezed her knee. "Any friend of Holly is a friend of mine."

I forced a grin and raised my glass. "Here's to great friends."

Holly chuckled, "I'll drink to that."

They both joined me in a toast, then I got up, glass in hand. "I'll take the rest of this upstairs. I feel much better now, and I've always believed that what goes around comes around. You never know, I may get a chance to get my own back one day."

Daniel gave a secretive smile and held his glass up again. "Let's hope so."

The following day, I pulled up next to a large van in front of the manor. Dashing inside, I found Tom in the kitchen and asked him about it. Obviously distracted, he muttered something about upgrading the security. His hands fumbled with the cups as he offered to make tea. Feeling his anxiety, I suggested he sat down while I made it myself.

I felt sorry for Tom. I guessed that Karl had made the arrangements and not even bothered to explain it to the poor man.

He picked at his fingernails. "Emily, I've got a proposition for you."

I stopped making the tea and turned around, raising my eyebrows in mock surprise. "How intriguing." I smiled, hoping I knew what he was going to say. *I hope he's going to ask me to live in. Karl thinks he's convinced him he has no interest in me. Tom will have to believe I'm safe, or it will never work.*

"I know you've been looking for a flat, and I could do with some more help, so I wondered if you would like to live here. As a friend and employee, that is." He blushed as he said this last bit.

Yes! It worked. I feigned surprise and concern. "Do you mind what people think, though? I know it's the twenty-first century, but your family might not approve." His anxiety skittered through me. *Is he afraid I'll say no? Poor Tom. I really don't want to deceive him. If only I could tell him the truth.*

"Oh, I don't care what other people think. But what do *you* think? I have a lot of work at the moment, and you said you hate your friend's new boyfriend. It's a perfect solution for us both. If you could cook dinner each evening, and do my washing and ironing, you can live here rent free. What do you say?"

He smiled, and I could have hugged him. Why was love so damn cruel? Any sane woman would love him and pray that friendship would turn to something more. I pictured Karl and continued with the plan.

"I should sleep in one of the old servant rooms."

"Why? I have plenty of rooms."

"Because you're my boss. It's only right."

"You can't sleep in the attic; I'm not even sure the floorboards are safe."

"What about the old nanny's room?" It was the other end of the house from Tom's room and right next to the old staircase, making it easier for me to move around without him knowing.

"If that will make you happy, it's fine by me. When would you like to move in?"

That night, I told Holly.

"Don't worry, you haven't got rid of me completely. We can still go out Wednesday and Saturday nights."

"Good, because I've already told Daniel those nights are sacred! How are you, though? Aren't you worried Karl will turn up again?"

"If he does, I'll tell Tom. I'm more angry than upset now. If I could get my own back in some way, I would."

I left it there and hoped this would be passed on to Daniel.

On Thursday night, Holly helped me pack up my few belongings. I nestled my treasured book into my suitcase.

Holly's eyes rested on the book. "*Wuthering Heights*... mmm... looks like an old copy. When did you get it? Must have cost a bit."

"It was a present."

"Oh?"

The *oh* hung like a question, but I chose not to answer it.

After a pause, she tilted her head. "I'll miss you living here, you know."

Her love should have warmed my insides, but her innocent eyes tugged at my conscience.

"Thanks, but you won't miss me tidying your things so you can't find them." I tried to joke, but even to me, it sounded hollow.

The doorbell rang. Holly went off to answer it, leaving me packing. A few minutes later, I descended the stairs with my suitcase to find her in the lounge standing beside Daniel. They both looked at me. I felt their uncertainty.

It was Holly who spoke first. "Emily, Daniel has something to tell you. You may want to sit down."

I looked from one to the other. "What? Just tell me."

They both sat down. I followed suit.

Daniel's blue eyes pierced into mine. "It's about Karl Ashton."

I put on my best anxious look, "Oh...What about him?"

Daniel looked at Holly and then back to me. "Look, Emily, I heard bad stuff about this guy. I had a friend in the force run his name through the database. Apparently, there are some big question marks around him in relation to some unsolved murders in Kent, ten years ago."

I did my best to look shocked. "So, why aren't the police after him?"

He frowned. "No evidence; they had to back off. But the cases are ongoing."

I noticed his jaw muscle twitching. Was he lying? Was Karl a suspect in these murder cases? Was he guilty? Was he being watched? An unwanted picture flashed into my head: a locked cupboard door. Did he have something incriminating in his quarters? What if the police issued a warrant to search? I pushed the thoughts from my head. Karl had come up with the plan. He must know the risks.

I put my head in my hands. "Oh my God! He seemed so honest about having a bad reputation and doing things he regretted... I thought he'd told me everything." I hit my head with my open hand. "What an idiot!"

Holly rushed to my side and put her arm around me. "Thank God he's gone, Emily. You could have been next."

I looked at Daniel. "The murders: were they women?"

"Yes. All about your age; all pretty."

"So, why am I still alive? Why did he go? He could have killed me several times."

"I don't know. Perhaps he was called away, but he may be back. Tell me everything you know about him and which hotel you met in. I'll help the police stop him killing anyone else."

I reeled off the story I'd rehearsed with Karl. Karl knew the Landlord of the *Country Retreat* on the outskirts of Taunton, and said he would fix it for him to say we had stayed there. Again, I had opted not to ask him his methods of persuasion.

I promised Daniel I would tell him if Karl contacted me again. I was sharply aware I had filled Holly with terror, and for that, I will always be truly sorry.

Trembling, she gripped my hands in anguish, "Don't move to the manor, Emily. What if he looks for you there?"

"One thing I'm sure of: he doesn't want Tom involved in whatever he's doing. I'll threaten to tell him...or the police. I'll call the police. And I promise I'll let Daniel know if I hear anything."

March...

I stood in front of Karl in his bedroom and told him how the plan had worked. But I hated myself. If only living in that gorgeous house, so close to the man I loved, had lived up to my childhood dreams. But how could it? How could I have imagined the fear of losing him or the pain of lying to my closest friends and my family?

I snapped. "It's okay for you to look smug, but I take no pleasure in any of it. You're not the one lying to your best friend. I'm following your orders with blind faith. I have to believe Daniel is the enemy, but the lines are blurred, and I wanted no part in deciding who lives and who dies." I sighed and shook my head. "Honestly, Karl, I don't think I can go through with setting Daniel up and destroying my friendship with Holly."

He turned away and paced the room. "I won't kill him unless I have to."

My mouth hung open. *Kill him?* "What?"

"I can see you're upset, and I get it. You don't want to cause someone's death. Well, you won't be. If he dies, it's his choice, not yours."

Fear climbed up my spine and lodged itself in my skull. "So, what are you planning to do?"

His eyes were cold. "Show him. Coming up against me is a mistake. I want him to know I'm always one step ahead; that I know all about his weapons and his team, and I still went to meet him. I'm stronger and smarter than him, and always will be. He needs to know; if he starts a war it won't just be him who regrets it. It will spread. Other vampires will join in; innocent people will die. First here in England, then who knows? News spreads." His eyes were cold.

I shivered as an icy hand gripped my heart. "You don't really want to start a global war against humans, do you?"

I think this was the first time I really understood what he was capable of and it terrified me. He suddenly sensed my fear and his eyes softened as he stepped closer to me, touching my arm.

"No, of course not," he said softly, touching my hair.

As he took my face gently in his hands, I looked up into his emerald eyes, searching for reassurance.

"He has to believe I would do anything, Emily. It's our best chance of getting him to back off and leave us alone." He kissed my hair and I leaned into him. "Then, we can be happy."

My reservations remained. "This isn't just about us, Karl."

"You said yourself he was using Holly. She'll be better off without him."

I sighed, wishing I had his confidence. I looked at the new security monitor he'd had fitted in his living area.

"It's very sophisticated," said Karl. "I didn't use the same firm that fitted the existing security system for Tom; I had a vampire in to do a proper job. Jimmy's lived his life as a thief. He knows all there is to know about security and how to get around it. Since he became a vampire, he's put his knowledge to good use, protecting his kind – for a fee of course."

His words should have made me feel better, but the winking light on the monitor only served as a reminder of the danger.

"What if they find a way to get to you with those new weapons? What if they can destroy you, and the other vampires? What if you lose?"

He pulled me over to an armchair, lifting me into his lap as he sat down.

"Lose? I'm not going to lose." He kissed me softly.

"How can you be so sure?"

"Prof found out they've developed a new UV bullet, but the guns themselves still rely on a human hand pulling the trigger. We can move faster than humans; we can move faster than bullets. They think they have the element of surprise, but they don't. We do."

Again, he soothed my fears with his words and his touch. He was my addiction, an opiate running through my veins. Only with him, each hit was as strong as the first, and I never came down from the high. I knew even then, that however bad he was for me, I would keep going back for more.

The next time Daniel called for Holly, I handed him a note;

I've missed you, Emily.
Meet me in the multi storey-car park
8 o clock Tuesday night

K xx

"He's unbelievable! He thinks he can just whistle, and I'll go running. Well, not this time." My heart hammered as I told another lie.

"Leave this to me," he said, studying the note.

"Don't you mean the police?"

"Look, I need to level with you. I'm on a special task force that helps the police in cases like this. I'll be with you the whole time."

My heart lurched. "You mean you want me to turn up!" I hadn't bargained on this. I thought he would just go there with his friends.

"He won't show himself unless he sees you. We need him to think everything is okay. You won't be any danger; we won't let him near you."

Won't let him near me! I bet he knows Karl can move like lightening, and there's nothing he can do to protect me! That's when I decided I hated him. With every pore of my being, I could feel he was lying. He wasn't concerned for my safety, or anyone else's. All he felt was pride, malice, arrogance and hatred. I pushed his feelings away, as they threatened to poison me.

My mind went back to the very first time I met him and felt the hairs on the back of my neck stand up. Why had I ever doubted or forgotten what I knew – that he was evil?

I knew he'd be perfectly fine with reporting me as collateral damage in his quest to kill Karl. And what for? To rid the world of an evil predator? No, I didn't believe so. If that were true, I would have picked up on some concern, some humility, and care, at least, some feelings for his friends or colleagues, but no. He was looking for glory for himself and if others got hurt, so be it.

There was coldness in Daniel, far more sinister than anything I'd ever felt from Karl. Karl didn't pretend to be something he wasn't. Daniel did. I felt a darkness in him like pure evil.

I am telling you this because I want you to understand. Karl was not the monster. Not to me. Not ever. Any doubt I had evaporated in that moment. All Karl wanted was a chance to be happy, to be loved. If people like Daniel left him alone, he wouldn't hurt anyone. He had no need to.

Karl wasn't looking for war, but if there was to be one, I suddenly knew whose side I was on.

K9

I glanced into my rear-view mirror. The back looked empty, but I knew Daniel lay across the seat clutching a pistol loaded with UV bullets.

I had relayed everything I knew to Karl, but my stomach flipped over as I pulled into the multi-storey car park. Other vampire hunters had arrived before dusk and positioned themselves ready to destroy a vampire. My vampire. I gripped the steering wheel tighter to stop my hands from shaking.

I heard a ping as Daniel received a text.

"My men are in position," he said cheerfully. "No sign of Karl Ashton yet."

His enthusiasm made my stomach lurch.

I didn't want to consider what could go wrong. I concentrated on tuning into Daniel's feelings. He wasn't even nervous. He was excited.

"Get out of the car," Daniel ordered. "Make sure he sees you."

I shuddered from revulsion and fear. With my heart thundering inside my chest, I opened the door and climbed out. I blinked, scanning the lines of parked cars in the gloom. Tension ran up my spine, escaping me in a small gasp, as the car door slammed behind me. Please be careful, Karl, I prayed silently. I took a few steps from the car and waited, suddenly aware of the heavy silence. My skin prickled.

I checked my watch; it was eight 'o' clock. Hearing footsteps, I held my breath. Karl stepped out from behind a van and stood in the aisle.

"Emily." As he spoke, his eyes searched the shadows around me.

For a moment, I froze, then I remembered our plan and ran in the opposite direction. I dropped to my knees and crawled between two cars. Feeling the cold concrete through my jeans, I braced myself for gunshots.

Nothing. Nothing but the blood pulsing in my ears.

I peered around the side of the car and saw Karl standing perfectly still. *Listening?* The icy grip of fear tiptoed up my spine and jangled every nerve in my body. *Where the hell is Daniel?*

Suddenly, my adrenaline pumped even harder. I felt excitement and determination as if I wanted this battle to commence. I frowned, as my fear broke through in a prickly rash and my heart missed a beat. The feelings weren't all mine. I sensed evil. And it came from behind me.

As I tried to shout to Karl, a hand clamped over my mouth, and a knife pressed against my throat.

Karl heard my muffled cry and was in front of the cars in a second. Daniel dragged me to my feet, the knife never losing its bite. Karl's face was set in a snarl, made more menacing by the dull yellow glow of the car-park lighting. I felt his anger twisting inside me, mixed with Daniels triumph and my fear. It was a sickening cocktail. Karl backed up a couple of steps when he saw the knife.

Daniel chuckled. "So, you do care about her. I hoped you did. It gives me another way to hurt you." He took his hand from my mouth and thrust the gun over my shoulder. Then, he slowly nudged me into the aisle.

Karl made a noise in his throat that was more animal than human. Unable to move, with a blade against my neck, I watched his eyes turn red.

Daniel sneered. "Are you sure you want to change in front of your girlfriend?"

Karl looked at me, then took a step back. "If you hurt her, I swear I will torture you every day for the rest of your life."

Daniel's laugh trailed off; a flash of fear ran through him, heightening my own.

Now it was Karl who laughed. "Waiting for anyone?" he snarled, reaching into his pocket and pulling out a phone. "Thanks for the text, by the way."

Daniel tightened his grip on me, his short breaths warming my neck.

"You bitch!" He yelled in my ear. "You told him everything didn't you? Talk about sleeping with the enemy."

With the blade on my throat, I couldn't move.

"Where the hell are my men!" he shouted to Karl.

Karl darted forward. "Before you do anything stupid, your friends aren't dead yet, but they will be if you hurt her. You may as well put the pistol down; I'm wearing bullet-proof clothes, and there's no way you'll get a head shot and hold on to her." He leapt through the air, spinning and landing on his feet behind us.

Daniel twisted me around with him to face Karl. I winced as I felt the sting of the blade.

"Tell me what you've done with them, or I'll kill her."

"Easy," Karl growled, "they weren't expecting humans to drug them in broad daylight. All it took was a hotdog stand and a pretty girl. I had them tied up and bundled into that van over there." He jerked his thumb behind him. "They should wake up soon. Let her go and I'll give you the keys, otherwise, I'll go over there and send them to sleep permanently."

I felt Daniel's mood darken, his anger mixing with humiliation.

"Send them to sleep permanently? I'm sure you're more than willing to add more murders to your record. Anyway, men are easily replaced."

Karl pulled the van keys from his pocket and dangled them from his finger.

"Not quickly enough to get you out of here alive." Karl pulled the van keys from his pocket and dangled them from his finger. I hope you don't mind, but my friends took all their weapons."

"You have human friends? Don't make me laugh."

"Well, pets really. Some like to serve, some like to bleed, some hope to become one of us. They're very useful."

I winced, even though I knew Karl was goading him. His words were hard to hear.

"I hope you're hearing this, Emily! Do you like being a pet?" Daniel lowered the pistol but kept the knife tight to my throat.

I closed my eyes against tears, as the sting of the knife bit into me. But I could sense Daniel's hesitance.

"How do I know you won't kill me as soon as I let her go?"

"If you live this night, it's because I promised Emily I wouldn't kill you. I'm not making promises beyond tonight. One thing you can be certain of; if you hurt Emily you won't see tomorrow."

Daniel's uncertainty invaded me. His grip relaxed and I took a deep breath, relieved that the knife lost its bite on my neck.

"She walks to the van with me."

"You have ten seconds to let her go." Karl didn't relent.

Daniel pulled me back towards the van, keeping his eyes on Karl, who followed a few paces behind, counting as he walked.

"One, two, three, four, five, six…"

"Okay, throw me the keys and I'll let her go."

"Drop the gun first."

Daniel threw the gun on the floor and kicked it towards Karl. "Now the keys."

Karl threw the keys and Daniel shoved me towards him. For a split second, I felt something was wrong, but Karl scooped me up in his arms before I had a chance to think. As he hugged me to him, I heard Daniel laughing.

"Get in the car," Karl whispered in my ear.

He released me and I took a few steps backwards, but my eyes were transfixed on both men. I hadn't noticed Daniel move, but he held a black bar in his hand. My blood ran cold as Karl's face began to transform. Even from the side, I could see his features elongate and his eyes narrow, then he launched himself through the air. Heart pumping, I held my breath, expecting Daniel to fall.

There was a strange violet glow, then Karl howled in pain, falling to his knees.

What happened? I think I knew straight away, but didn't want to acknowledge it. As I dashed to Karl, I heard Daniel running away. Pain seared through my heart as I knelt close to him. His hands were shielding his face from me. Putting my arm around his shoulders, I cried out, as the pain slammed into me even harder.

"UVA light," he whispered. His breath came in deep rasps.

Gritting my teeth against the pain, I peered through the gloom. I watched Daniel's back receding. He was heading for the van and his men. *I've got to get a grip before he sets them free.* "Karl!" I yelled, grabbing his arm. "Come on, we have to get out of here!"

I helped him stand and led him to the car, wondering how I would drive while I could feel his pain. I opened the passenger door and helped him in. He didn't take his hands away from his face, but I had seen pictures of burns victims; my stomach churned thinking about it.

I sat in the driver seat, trying to compose myself. Tears ran down my face, and my hands shook as I tried to put the key in the ignition. I tried to slow my breathing as panic threatened to immobilise me. "What if they follow us?"

"Flat tires." Karl croaked.

Pain ripped through me as if it were my own. He must have realised because it suddenly stopped.

"You don't have to do that," I said.

"Yes, I do."

"Will you heal?"

"Yes." It was almost a whisper, but it gave me the strength to drive us home.

I switched off the engine and turned to him. "Karl, I don't know how to get you inside without Ned or Tom seeing us together."

The clock in the car said 9:15. I couldn't believe so little time had passed since I had left to pick Daniel up.

"Leave the car near the garage with the door unlocked. I'll manage."

"Are you sure? Why don't you stay in the car and I'll come back out when Tom's asleep."

"No. Please leave me. I mean it."

He was still hiding his face from me, and I knew he wanted to be alone.

I left him, wishing he would trust me enough to let me help him. Inside, I managed to hold it together while I spoke to Tom. I told him I had a headache and went up to bed.

Alone, my fear chilled me to the bone. With no one to turn to, I fell onto the bed, sobbing.

I crawled under the covers, fully clothed, but couldn't sleep. I worried about Karl, worried about Holly, and worried about Tom. The hunters were alive and knew where we were. I hoped this meant there would be no need to use Holly anymore. Should I warn her? Was I wrong to make Karl promise not to kill Daniel? What if he attacked at dawn?

The clock said 4:12. Throwing off the duvet, I pulled my boots on, tugged a coat on, grabbed a torch, and then quietly left my room. Not wanting to wake Tom by passing his room,

I went to the servants' stairs. Karl had given me a key, but this was the first time he hadn't been there to meet me and guide me. I felt alone.

The torch shook in my hand, making it harder to see, but I kept going until I reached the ground floor. Karl had taken me through the cellar, into the passage underground, but the door had always been unlocked. I tried the handle, but it refused to budge. *What now?*

I would have to go through the woods. Hopefully, I'd find my way to the steps in the ground.

Hurrying to the back door, I came to a halt as I saw the flashing light winking on the panel. *Damn the alarm!*

Tom had given me the security number, but my mind went blank. Then I remembered; it was a famous year. I typed in 1666, year of the great fire of London. The light turned green, and I walked into the cold night air.

I soon found my way to Toby's grave. I remembered the oak tree and the way the roots broke out of the earth in places. There were crocuses there, and I remembered that winter had turned to spring. My mind returned to the day I had followed the arrows. One by the oak tree and one by the tree stump. I squinted my eyes to see better in the weak torchlight and realised I was at the place where the ground sloped downward and the brambles grew thicker. I searched closely for a break in the bramble – *there! I've found it*. I knelt in the damp earth and felt for the cord to lift the hatch. It was heavier to lift than I had imagined. Struggling, I managed to open it and get inside. By the time I stood outside of Karl's door I was aching and filthy.

I banged on the door, even though I knew his CCTV security system would have picked me up several times. I waited, staring up at the camera.

He obviously wasn't in a hurry to let me in. I panicked for a moment. Maybe he hadn't made it inside himself, or he was too hurt to get to the door. "Karl", I shouted, "if you can hear me, please let me in. I'm worried Daniel will attack in the morning, and you'll be defenceless. Please. At least, tell me what you want me to do."

I waited again. Still nothing. He had to be in there, he just had to be.

"Karl! I'm tired and filthy and scared half to death, so if you're ignoring me out of pride, because of your face, I'm going to be really pissed off!" My words were brave, but I trembled with cold and fear. I banged the door, then stamped my foot in frustration. Finally, I sunk to the floor and cried until my eyes hurt.

Eventually, the door swung open beside me.

I pulled myself up to my feet, wiping my eyes with my sleeve, then jumped in surprise as I looked at the stranger.

"What's the matter? Never seen a black man before?" His voice was deep, almost gruff, and his shoulders were broad. He wasn't handsome, but he held himself with such confidence that it was hard to look away. Shrinking a little inside, I raised my chin and pulled my shoulders back, trying to look more confident than I felt. "I haven't seen a black vampire before."

His dark eyes narrowed. "How do you know I'm a vampire?"

"You hide your feelings too well to be human, and judging by your face, you have the same mixture of anger, amusement and exasperation I'm used to."

He raised one eyebrow and peered down at me; a slight smile playing around his lips. "Mmm, Karl said you're smart. I suppose you thought we were all pale and beautiful?"

"I'm not prejudiced if that's what you're implying; I just wasn't expecting to see anyone else here."

"He also said you're stubborn and quick with a sharp tongue."

I felt a mixture of anger, concern and love as I imagined him saying exactly that.

"Where is he? I want to see him. Is he okay?"

The stranger sighed. "He's resting. He's healing, but you're not seeing him in the state you're in! Do you really think crying and wailing outside his door will help him?"

"Why did you let me in if you're not going to let me see him? And who the hell are you anyway?" I refused to let him intimidate me. This was too important.

"I'm Prof, and I let you in because he told me to."

I smiled in triumph and walked towards the bedroom. *So this is Prof. Can't say I like him much, but I guess he's trying to do the right thing.*

"He also told me to ask you to leave him alone for a few more days. He needs to finish healing."

I stopped, deflated. Then spun around to face him. "What about the vampire hunters? They could attack during the day. They know where he lives."

"We haven't survived so long by being stupid. Plenty of humans are loyal to us. As soon as I heard what happened last night I sent word to them and other vampires across the country. During the day, our human friends will keep watch. Other vampires are making their way through the tunnels as we speak and yet more will travel tonight. They will not beat us."

As I listened, my heart raced. Is this the global war starting? "I need to speak to Karl. Now!"

His face hardened. "No. You need to leave."

I stood firm, with only a few feet between us and steel in my voice. "Last night, I was held at knife-point. I could have been killed. I'm glad Karl is healing, and I'm glad he has protection, but what about me? I'm involved! It was me who got Karl back her to safety on my own, and I've been awake ever since, worrying about him. I have found my way through

125

the wood and tunnels in the dark, and now I need to see him. There's no one else I can talk to about any of this. There's no one else I *want* to talk to."

He scowled and folded his arms.

"If I'm in a state, so be it. I've never expected Karl to apologise for who and what he is, and I will not apologise for who and what I am. If you want me to leave you will have to throw me out."

I kept my voice steady, but inside my emotions were boiling.

Prof clenched his fists. I could feel spikes of anger breaking through his control. "If it's safety you seek, why not go back and live with your friend. If you're looking for emotional comfort, I doubt you will find it here."

"You know nothing of us. If Karl wants me gone, he can come out and tell me himself."

"I know enough to know you're not doing him any good. It was you being there that messed up everything. Karl would have killed that hunter, but he ended up getting hurt trying to protect you!"

"You think I wanted to be there?" I yelled. "I'm risking my life in this. If it wasn't for me, he wouldn't have known about the vampire slayers at all!"

He took a step towards me. "You're his Achilles heel. You stop him using his anger."

"Then maybe I'm his strength!" I squared my shoulders and held my ground.

"That's enough!"

We both turned at the sound of Karl's voice behind us. He was wearing dark glasses, and his face was still blistered in places, but it was nowhere near as bad as I had feared. I was so glad to see him, my anger evaporated immediately.

"Thank you, Prof, you can leave us."

He left without question.

I hesitated. Was Prof right? Should I have left him to rest? "I'm sorry Karl, but I had to check you were okay."

He held his arms out and I ran into them, holding him tightly.

"You have nothing to be sorry for, Emily."

As he stroked my hair, he opened his feelings to me. One emotion surprised me; shame.

K10

"Why do you feel shame?" I muttered into his chest, wanting to stay close to him.

"I let him outsmart me."

I shifted in his arms and looked up at him. "Oh, so this is about pride. You weren't to know about that light stick thing he had. And he didn't outsmart you. He went there to destroy you, and all he achieved was temporarily blinding you." I realised I'd made an assumption and fear gripped my heart. "It was temporary, wasn't it? Your eyes are healing?"

"Yes, but he walked away unharmed." He pulled away from me and looked down at the floor. There was clearly more to his feelings than he was letting through, but I knew better than to push him.

After a few moments, he spoke softly. "What you said to Prof was right. You could have been killed last night."

I felt the warmth of his love and took his hands in mine. "I'm fine. I was only angry that you shut me out. I was worried sick about you."

He squeezed my hands. "I'm so sorry. You could have died because of me and I'm not prepared to risk it again."

"Meaning what?" I couldn't see his eyes behind the dark lenses. It was disconcerting, like a missing connection.

"Meaning I want you to go and stay somewhere safe for a while."

"What! You agree with him. You think I'm a liability." Pain rose from my chest, threatening to choke me.

He pressed his lips against my hands, kissing them softly. "That's not true, but I don't want to be responsible for your death."

I stared at my reflection in his glasses. "What about what *I* want, Karl? I won't let you send me away again. I'm not a parcel to be sent off when I'm not needed." I blinked rapidly, feeling tears pricking the back of my eyes.

"It isn't like that, Emily."

His voice was gentle, but it didn't console me. The jagged shards of icy fear pierced the heat of my anger. My body began to tremble. "Please don't make me go."

"I don't want to, but I must. Perhaps Toby's death was just a terrible tragedy. Perhaps no one was to blame, but if you die here, because of what I am, it will be my fault."

"No, you're not making me stay; I choose to."

"I need you to trust me, Emily."

I was silent. *Do I trust him? Completely?* My eyes slid towards the locked cupboard door. "Then stop keeping secrets from me."

He turned to follow my gaze, then sighed, dropping my hands. "Why are you bothered about that cupboard? What exactly do you think I keep in it?"

Crossing my arms, I glared at him. "I have no idea, but I doubt it's linen."

He paused for a moment, staring at me, then fished in his pocket and pulled out a key. Handing it to me, he said, "Go on. Take a look."

His mouth was a straight line. I felt his anxiety give way to deep sadness.

Fingers trembling, I unlocked the door and then paused, looking back at him. He nodded.

My heart hammered in my chest. What did I expect to find? Pulling open the door, I peered into the dimly lit cupboard and took a step inside. Turning my head, I looked along shelves of toys and children's books. I reached out to touch a wooden train, then stopped and turned to Karl. "Are all these things Toby's?"

He nodded, and the grey emptiness of his grief washed over me. "I made that train for him, and the cars."

I hesitated. Was I making him confront his feelings? His grief seemed so fresh as if Toby had died recently. I hoped I could make it easier for him.

An oval frame on the bottom shelf caught my eye. I crouched down, but the light was too dim to see properly. I pointed, not daring to touch anything without Karl's permission. "Is that a portrait of him?"

"Yes." His voice caught slightly. "You can look at it if you want."

Picking up the small frame, I stepped from the cupboard and took Karl's hand, bracing myself against the strength of his feelings. "I'm sorry, love. I wish you had told me."

I cradled the oval portrait in my other hand, looking from the portrait to Karl. "He looks like you."

He hooked an arm around me and crushed me to his chest. "I'm sorry I lied. Sometimes forgetting is easier."

"Is it?" I gripped his back with my free hand and gritted my teeth as his torment soaked into me.

"No. Not really. And Toby should never be forgotten." He pulled away and held my face in his hands. "You're my salvation, Emily. Can't you see I need you? I won't send you away for a moment longer than I need to, but I can't bear the thought of your things in that cupboard next to his."

He pressed his lips to mine, and I knew I would have to go away.

I stood, clutching the portrait in my hand. With tears running freely, I reached up and pulled his sunglasses from his face. His eyebrows were gone, and some of his black lashes, but his eyes were still beautiful.

Standing on tiptoes, I gently kissed the red skin on his face, then looked into his eyes. "Where will I go? I can't stay at Holly's." I reasoned. "I don't even know what to say to her. Either Daniel will tell her I betrayed him, or he just won't turn up again. Either way, she'll be upset with me for involving him in my life."

"You can't stay there anyway. I don't want them thinking they can use you as bait. You need to go somewhere they can't find you."

"Where then?"

He kissed my hair. "I know somewhere safe. I'll arrange it tonight. You need to leave first thing tomorrow."

I crumpled against him. How could my heart be swelling with love, and breaking at the same time?

"It's for your safety, Emily, and it won't be for long. You should go back upstairs now before Tom wakes up. Tell everyone you need a holiday. Say you're just going to drive and find hotels along the way. I want you to drive out of town to Ryerton and go into the church. Someone will meet you there at ten-thirty. That will give you enough time to pack and make your excuses. The person I send will ask you if you're seeking sanctuary."

"But how far am I going, and how will I know if you're okay?" I clung to him. His sorrow twisted with mine and settled deep in my belly.

"I'll be okay, knowing you're safe. Please, you must go."

Reluctantly, I nodded and pulled away. I looked at the portrait of Toby. "I'll put this back."

"Wait. Keep it with you. Look after it for me."

His gesture of trust, and the love I felt pouring into my poor battered heart, gave me the strength to walk away. Looking down at the portrait of Toby, so like his father, I wiped a fallen tear from the glass with my finger. I had no idea when I would see Karl again.

The following morning, Tom guessed I was leaving. I could feel disappointment and pain hitting me in short bursts before I'd even told him. He swallowed my lie and managed to wish me a great holiday, then helped me put my bags in the car. I imagined the picture of Toby, nestled safely between my clothes. I hoped I could return it to Karl soon.

"Take care, Emily," he said, placing a hand on my shoulder.

With my feelings in turmoil, I left to call in on Holly and say goodbye.

Like Tom, she knew straight away that something was wrong. I told her about my holiday. I also told her that Daniel was using her to hurt Karl, giving her a potted version of events the night before.

"I'm sorry, Holly, but we were just pawns in their game." I didn't have the guts to tell her I was part of it. I soaked up as much of her pain, humiliation and anger as I could without losing my mind. I was already feeling the burden of Karl's shame and anger entwined with my own. I wondered how much more I could take.

I shivered as I entered the tiny stone church and sat in a pew at the back. Looking up at the stained glass window, I wondered if I should pray. Did I have any right? If there was truly a God, how much could he forgive? Had I already gone too far?

"My intentions are good!" I said, to nobody in particular. I hoped that if God heard, he understood. The door opened quietly behind me. I stood looking towards it, afraid and curious. I couldn't have been more surprised when a young man's voice said, "Are you looking for sanctuary?"

I realised I hadn't answered him when he flushed with embarrassment and turned away from me.

"I'm sorry. I mean yes. Yes, I am. I was expecting someone older."

I felt his annoyance and regretted my words.

"I'm eighteen, which makes me an adult, the same as you."

I felt his pride boiling and noticed the defiance in his eyes. He was tall and thin, and stooped over as if embarrassed by his own body. He kept glancing at me and glancing away, clearly annoyed. Wanting to win him over, I grinned. "Actually, I'm twenty-one, so I'm practically ancient compared to you."

His spotty face gave way to a small smile, and I could tell for a moment he could be good looking if he lost the spots and gained some confidence. He jerked his head in the direction of the door and walked out. I followed, pulling my suitcase behind me.

"You can leave your car here. I'll move it later."

I got into his battered Ford, wrinkling my nose as the smell of sweat and food cartons hit me.

We set off in silence. My early attempts at conversation met with a disapproving frown. Not one to give up easily, I tried again. "How did you come to be helping me?"

"Lord Ashton told me to. No way am I going to ignore him."

I assumed he was talking about Karl. "I meant, how did you come to know about him?"

He rolled his eyes. "He didn't tell me I had to answer a load of questions."

"Sorry, I was just wondering."

His eyes were fixed on the road ahead. "How come you're so special? Not like him to want some human protected."

I was getting tired of his attitude. It wasn't as if I wanted to go on this journey. "He didn't tell me I had to answer your questions either," I snapped.

I soon regretted my abruptness. The silence was worse than his moodiness, especially as I could still feel his annoyance. It was like having a constant itch that I couldn't reach to scratch.

We drove for hours and I tried to keep track of where we were, but we rarely kept to main roads and the signposts on the country lanes were few.

Pulling into a lay-by, my companion glanced my way. "Refreshment time." He got out and rummaged in the back. A packet of sandwiches came over my shoulder and landed in my lap.

"Thanks." I caught his eye and smiled. "What's your name?" I asked, suddenly realising I didn't know.

He got back in the driving seat and handed me a bottle of water.

"Scott."

He looked away, but it was a start. As we ate, rain started to tap against the windows, until the tapping became a loud drumming sound. I stared at a gate and winced. "Sorry, but I need to pee." Without looking at him, I turned up the collar of my coat and braved the rain. I climbed over the padlocked gate and found privacy behind the hedge.

Scott looked as sullen as ever when I returned to the car, but I saw him look at my dripping wet hair and could feel his amusement, so I scowled at him.

A couple more hours driving and I was surprised to see the sea in the distance. Normally, it would have been a welcome sight, but the rain was pelting down, and the sea looked grey and angry.

Actually, the whole world looked grey and angry.

After driving down a very long narrow track, we arrived at an old farmhouse, and Scott stopped the car. He got out, but I just sat and stared in disbelief. The house looked deserted and run down; the outbuildings were falling down and the garden couldn't be seen for junk. Great! Just what I needed.

A rap on the passenger window startled me.

"Come on then," he shouted.

To my surprise, he took my suitcase from the boot and carried it inside.

I looked again at the site in front of me. Was this it?

Inside, the house wasn't any more appealing than the outside. I glanced at the dirty pots and pans all over the kitchen. *How many rats have made this their home?*

Scott must have guessed my thoughts. He shrugged. "Didn't have time to clean up. Don't worry, you won't be here long."

The relief probably showed on my face, but I didn't care. "How long?"

"Just till dark, then we take the boat out. I don't want to risk anyone following, but I'll still find the way. I know every inch of this coastline."

"Oh. Is this your place?"

"Yeah."

"Do you live here on your own?"

"Yeah."

I could see that conversation was still going to be difficult.

He gestured towards the next room. "You can sit in there if you want. I can make coffee."

I looked at the filthy mugs. He followed my gaze, then rummaged under the sink and came up with washing up liquid.

"Yes, that would be nice. Thanks."

Satisfied that he was washing the mugs, I dragged my suitcase through to the living room. It was a good-sized room with an open fireplace. There was a hotchpotch of furniture, which looked old and unloved. But at least the room was tidy. I wondered if he ever used it.

I knelt on the floor and opened the front pocket of my case. I was looking for my new paperback but saw the scarf wrapped around my copy of *Wuthering Heights*. I eased the bundle out, placed it on my lap and unwrapped the book.

It wasn't the book itself I wanted to read, but the notes I'd tucked inside. I had kept every word Karl had sent to me. He never wrote much. In fact, a couple just had *xxxxxxx K* written on them, but they meant the world to me.

I know it doesn't seem like much, but I knew he'd never done anything like it for anyone else, ever. I didn't hear Scott walk in behind me. I felt his surprise and turned.

He spoke quickly, "You can say what you like. There must be something special about you if they're from him."

I quickly shoved the notes back into the book and put it away.

"I've never felt special." I thought about the notes again "But maybe I should. Karl seems to think so, though I don't know why."

"Does it matter why? All I know is even the vampires around here are scared shitless of him. Except for one."

"You mean Ana, I take it." I curled my lip at the thought of her snake-like charm.

"You know about her?" His surprise spiked again. I assumed he knew she'd been Karl's lover.

"I've met her. How come she isn't afraid of him? From what I've heard, sleeping with women hasn't always stopped him killing them. Is it just the human ones he's destroyed?"

Scott's mouth hung wide open. "You don't mind being blunt, do you!"

I shrugged. "I know about Karl, even the bits I'd rather not know. I don't know about Ana. Tell me."

"She's Benedikte's sister, and he sired Karl."

"What has that got to do with it?"

"Benedikte is a first blood, one of the original vampires. It gives him seniority and superior strength. I'm not saying Karl is afraid of him, from what I've heard they get on well, but he would think twice about hurting his sister."

"Where is Benedikte?"

"I don't know. I haven't heard about him for a while. I think he went back to Romania, but Ana stayed." He looked away.

I felt fear. It prickled up my spine. "Is something wrong?"

"You won't tell him I was rude to you will you? I didn't realise you meant something to him. I didn't think anyone meant anything to him."

I grinned, hoping I could make Scott an ally. "Were you rude? I hadn't noticed."

There was that smile again, but more importantly, his feelings changed instantly. I felt his relief mixed with a touch of respect.

He found some biscuits, and we drank our coffee in silence. He switched the television on and we half watched that and half watched the fading light at the window. As the sky got darker, he switched the television off and announced it was time to go.

The rain was light, but the ground was slippery. I lost my footing several times as we followed a narrow path to the pebble beach below. My heart sank when I saw a small fishing boat tethered half-in, half-out of the water.

"You climb in and I'll push her out," Scott called over his shoulder.

I clambered on-board as Scott threw his shoes and socks over the edge. Then I watched through the fading light, as he rolled up his trousers and untied the boat. He heaved it into the water with me clinging to the side. *He must be stronger than he looks.*

Once afloat, I sat in the small cabin and Scott started the motor. He joined me in the cabin and steered us out of the bay, into open sea. I was cold, wet and afraid, but took comfort in the confidence that Scott felt.

"How long will it take?" I raised my voice over the engine.

"About thirty minutes." He said, his eyes scanning the coastline through the dusk.

After a moment's pause, he replied, "It was my sister."

I was confused. "What was?"

"You asked how I knew about Karl. My sister is a vampire."

"Really?"

"Yes, really."

"Oh... does she live near you?"

"I haven't seen her for a while. She went away. That's why I'm helping. I don't like what she is, but she's my sister. I don't want her destroyed; she's all the family I have."

His sadness moved me.

"What's her name?"

"Amber. She was my big sister, but now she'll always be fourteen. I wish she'd come back. I thought about becoming one of them, but I'm not sure. I can't think about eternity. It seems like too long."

"I guess so. I hadn't thought."

"Hasn't Lord Ashton tried to talk you into it?"

"No." There was no reaction from Scott, as he manoeuvred expertly through the waves. A sudden lurch of the boat threw me sideways off the chair. I clutched the side of the boat.

"Are you okay?" Scott asked, as I scrambled to my feet.

"I think so," I said, thinking about his previous question. *What if Karl does ask me to become a vampire?* A wave of horror gripped me. *Why hadn't it even occurred to me?* I pushed the thought away; I had enough to worry about. "I don't think I want to be immortal."

Up ahead, a small light flickered in the distance. As we got nearer, I could make out a small jetty. Scott threw a rope over, then jumped across and moored the boat. The light I had seen was a lantern, which Scott picked up. All I could see was a small beach and a high cliff.

"Where on earth are we going?"

He faced me and jerked his thumb over his shoulder. "This way"

I looked at the cliff and gulped.

K11

I scurried along behind Scott, who was heading straight for the cliff. "Wait! Where are we going?" Fear stabbed at my heart while my mind whirled in confusion. The need to stay with another person drove me forward.

"Up," he responded, without turning.

He began to climb before me. Squinting in the dim light, I saw steps cut into the cliff. They were ridiculously steep, and I steadied myself against the wall as I followed him. Panting, I got to the top and bent over, waiting for my heart to stop banging against my ribs.

"This is as far as I go," Scott informed me. He put my case and the lantern down, and stepped aside for me to pass.

My mouth dropped open as fear clutched at my throat. "You can't leave me here!" I pleaded. "Where *is* here?"

"You'll be fine, Emily." He spoke softly. "Welcome to Sanctuary."

What? For a moment, I was stunned. *He's leaving me here?*

While my senses caught up with me, he disappeared back down the cliff steps. "Scott!" I wanted to follow him, but my legs held me rooted to the spot. The temperature seemed to plummet as the adrenaline which carried me that far deserted me. Holding the lantern in front of me, I tried to see in the dimpsy light. I could make out a gravel path, but no more.

I picked up my case and struggled up the path with my heart in my mouth and my eyes full of tears. Soon, a stone building loomed before me. Through misty eyes, I could see a couple of robed figures. I shuddered and hesitated.

"Emily?"

"Yes," I croaked, unnerved that their faces were hidden.

The figures moved towards me, lowering their hoods.

As they approached, I became aware of a change inside me. My heart slowed and the heavy feeling in my chest lifted. As their faces came into focus, I could see their smiles and feel calm wash over me, like a soothing balm for my soul.

One of them held out a hand. "Welcome to Sanctuary, Emily. I'm Brother Michael and this is Brother Peter."

The clanging bells woke me at five and I groaned aloud, just as I had for the past five days. I could picture brothers Michael and Peter putting on their robes ready for early morning Vigils. I rolled over to catch another hour of sleep before breakfast, but it evaded me.

Every waking hour was torture. I felt alone. Cut off from everything I knew. My mind teased me with hideous scenarios; awful things happening to Karl. The vice around my chest tightened another notch as I thought of my lover. *Is he okay?*

I washed, dressed and stumbled downstairs to the dining room, vaguely aware of smiles and good morning murmurs from the other residents tucking into breakfast. Everything I did was like moving through thick fog. I had to concentrate hard just to put one foot in front of the other.

Having finished their prayers, the Monks took their places beside me. "Will you join us for Lauds this morning, Emily?" brother Michael asked me quietly. He had asked me the same yesterday, and the day before. I forced my mouth to smile.

Lauds was the second service of the day, a time to celebrate the light of a new day and victory over evil. I wasn't convinced there had been any victory. Night would still come with its shadows. Evil still lurked. I wasn't even sure what evil was anymore. The lines had become blurred.

"I don't know, Michael. If there is a god, and I really want to believe there is, I don't think he will answer my prayers."

"Why not?"

"Because I would be praying for a vampire."

"You wouldn't be the first to pray for a sinner and be heard, Emily."

"I know you mean well, Michael, but if God can hear me he already knows what I want. I don't see that kneeling on a cold floor will help anyone."

I immediately felt pity in stereo.

"And you don't need to pity me. I will join you at work, I promise."

They both smiled and nodded their understanding. I looked along the big oak table, scanning the others as they chatted or sat quietly, sipping coffee or eating.

There were eight of us in total, all misfits who needed sanctuary. The calm and love I felt warmed me, like a favourite blanket. Only Moira, the eldest of the women, held some suspicion and fear. She tried to conceal it, but it was there. I kept out of her way.

Pushing my porridge around with a spoon, my mind drifted to Karl again. "I should have heard something by now," I said, to no one in particular.

"Scott will bring the boat in later. Perhaps he'll have news?" Lily said, her elfin face smiling from across the table.

I returned her smile, hoping she was right. I liked Lily. Apart from the monks, she was the only one I'd chatted with. I guessed she was about the same age as me, and her smile was infectious. During the last few days, I'd helped her in the monastery gardens. It kept me busy, which I was glad of, but I kept thinking about the garden I'd planted at Kenwood, which just reminded me of Karl. Not that I needed reminding.

Lily told me she had visions. Sometimes of the present, sometimes the future. Branded a freak by her so-called mates, she'd sought sanctuary. I was glad of her company. She helped me feel slightly less alone.

"I don't suppose you've *seen* anything, Lily? About Karl, I mean, or Kenwood." I felt the room quieten as everyone looked in my direction.

Lily shook her head. "I told you, it's totally random. I wish I could help."

I shrugged my shoulders, and the low chatter continued around the table.

"I'll help you outside again this morning if that's okay?" I was relieved when Lily nodded her agreement. I was desperate to keep busy, or I'd go stir crazy waiting for the boat.

The others gradually left the table, taking their plates and cups to the kitchen.

"You could kill some time getting to know them," Michael said, before following Peter with his plate.

I sighed and rolled my eyes at Lily. "He keeps on about me making friends with everyone, but I don't see the point. I don't plan on being here long."

"You don't have to become best mates with them. Just chat to them."

"You too, eh? I'll try to be friendlier. I'm sure they're all great." *They just aren't Karl.* I stood and picked up my things before Lily could see the tears in my eyes, but she wasn't fooled.

"I'm sure he'll be fine. From what I've heard, he's survived a very long time."

"Can you read my mind?"

"No, not me. It's obvious. You look so afraid."

I looked down. "It isn't myself I fear for."

"Isn't it? Aren't you afraid of losing him and being alone?" Her eyes regarded me with curiosity.

"Yes, I suppose so. Love is selfish, isn't it?"

"Not always, I hope."

What was that I felt from her? Love? For who? I wondered as I pushed the kitchen door open with my shoulder. Catching sight of the Brothers kissing, I recoiled, letting the door click shut. I gaped at Lily. *Do I pretend I didn't see them?*

"What's up with you?" she asked

"I, ah... Nothing."

She laughed. "Were the brothers kissing again?"

"Um..."

"It's okay; they do it all the time."

"They do?"

"That's why they set up this place; different from the other monasteries. They allow their kind of love here. Don't have to be celibate to love God, that's their theory. Actually, I think it's great." She looked at me, her blue eyes waiting for my reaction.

I let out a sigh of relief. "Good for them. Someone could have warned me, though!"

For a few moments, the weight on my heart lifted a little, but only a little.

We passed Callum on our way out to the garden. He nodded a greeting, a slight smile on his lips.

I checked he was out of earshot. "What does he do with himself?"

She grinned. "Why don't you ask him?"

I groaned. "Can't you just tell me about everyone? You know, give me the heads up."

"Heads up about what? What do you want to know?"

I realised I wasn't sure, but I was reluctant to approach Moira or Callum. Tyler seemed okay when I saw him. He didn't seem to do much, though. Kept himself to himself most of the time.

"Callum seems a bit scary," I ventured. "And Moira's doesn't like me. I can tell."

"Of course, Moira likes you, silly. She's just wary of strangers. She'll come around." She stopped as we got to the greenhouse, pulled several bean seed packets from her pocket and looked up at the blue sky. "It looks like spring is finally here. But we'll plant these under cover in case there's another frost."

I followed her inside. "What about Callum?"

She chuckled. "Oh, Callum. Is it the shaved head that scares you? He can look a bit fierce."

"It's not the hair, or lack of it. He just seems to look serious most of the time. Even when he smiles, it's just the merest hint. Have I pissed him off?"

She laughed again, handing me some pots and beans. "No. He always looks serious, but he's a dear, really."

I raised my eyebrows.

"Honestly, he is. Speak to him yourself and see."

"Okay, okay, I will. Sometime." I stabbed my trowel into the compost bag and started planting.

I planted, weeded, pruned, and did as Lily suggested all morning. I was moving on automatic, my mind elsewhere completely. *Is Tom still at the house? Surely, he'd be in danger too. Karl would ask him to leave. Wouldn't he? How did Karl know about this place? Why doesn't he contact me or visit me? What's happening?*

I found myself standing, looking at a basket of eggs in my hand. I had no recollection of entering the chicken coup, but the state of my shoes told me I had.

"Emily" Michael's voice cut through my thoughts, and I realised he was standing next to me with Peter. I caught my breath in surprise, nearly dropping the egg basket.

"Sorry, I was miles away."

Michael chuckled, his jowls shaking slightly. "I just wondered if you wanted a sandwich. You've been working hard this morning."

"No thanks, I'm not hungry."

They frowned in unison. Before they could chastise me for not eating, I asked, "How does Karl know about sanctuary? Has he been here?" A spike of fear made me gasp as I looked at their horrified faces.

Peter's small frame stepped from behind Michael's larger one. "He can't come here, Emily. He's too..." He faltered, looking at Michael.

"Unpredictable," Michael chipped in. "I'm sure you can ask him how he knows about us soon. Now, come and sit down. You need a drink at least."

"But he doesn't hurt anyone, not anymore!" I was defiant. They were supposed to be forgiving. Weren't they?

I saw the nervous glance that passed between them.

"Emily," Peter said softly, "you can't possibly guarantee that. Besides, do you really think he would want to? Won't he want to defend his home?"

As I realised the truth in his words, my anger turned into despair. "I wish I'd been given that choice."

"Come on, Emily, there's much to be thankful for."

I found myself being propelled along by Michael's large arm around my shoulder. I plonked myself down on a bench in a shady corner and took a deep breath to calm my thoughts.

Peter poured me a glass of cold water, which I sipped as I peered up at a plaque on the wall.

Founded in 1130

"Wow, that's a long time ago. How long have you two been here?"

"Not as long as that!" Peter quipped.

I laughed in spite of myself.

"We heard about it from another monk. He was like us, if you know what I mean." He grinned and patted Michael's hand. "Said he'd denied his sexuality all his life, and ended up wondering if it had ever been God's wish. He encouraged us to start a new life and told us about a place he once visited when he was young. All but forgotten about, he said."

"How did he know about this place?"

"We don't know," Peter said. "He died the next day. We owe him so much."

The brothers looked about them, smiling, then at each other. Their love capturing me in its embrace for a moment.

"It was quite an adventure getting here, I can tell you." Michael laughed and the bench shook. "We tried to find it by land first, but the forests had been left un-managed, and we wandered around in circles until we were exhausted. We didn't think we would find it by sea either at first. The fisherman we paid to transport us had never heard of the place, but we persuaded him to try." He glanced at Peter, who was nodding. "We sailed up and down, up and down. Then, just as we were about to give up, we saw him." He stopped, eyes wide.

I leaned forward on the edge of the seat. "Who?"

"A man in a monks' robe, standing on the cliff top, looking out to sea. He looked like he was waving, so we asked the fisherman to leave us on the beach, and up we came. Twas a real shock, I tell you. The state of this place! Well, it was a long time ago." He leant back with a dreamy look in his eyes.

Open-mouthed and exasperated, I asked, "What about the monk you saw? Who was he?"

"No idea. We never found him. Tis a real mystery."

They went gooey eyed at each other again. I decided three was a crowd and wandered off.

Walking around the building, I found a tree stump and sat down. I thought about the monks and tried not to think about Karl. Would we ever get to being happy like the monks?

A noise startled me; I turned to see Arin carrying a basket of leaves.

"Penny for them!"

"Oh, I was just thinking about the monks finding this place."

He sat on the grass in front of me, tucking his legs under him. "It's weird about the monk on the cliff top. Do you think it was a ghost?"

I laughed. "I'm learning to keep an open mind about most things." I looked into the basket beside him. "What are the leaves for?"

Arin was Sanctuary's cook and I was curious about what I might be seeing on my plate later.

"They're dandelion leaves, good for lots of things, but in this case to ward off gallstones. Peter suffers from them something bad, or he used to before he met me."

I looked at his dark eyes and sinewy frame. He was made for outdoors. "Can I ask you something?"

"Sure. Go ahead."

"Are you from Romania?"

"No, I was born in England. I've always lived here, but my mother was a Romanian gypsy. She taught me the ways of the land. This is the first place I've stayed for more than a year."

"And your mother?"

He looked at his hands. "Died in childbirth when I was fifteen. My sister was stillborn."

I reached out and put my hand on his arm. "I'm so sorry."

We sat in silence for a minute or so.

He looked up, smiling shyly, his brown eyes bright. "I like it here. I don't really fit in anywhere out there." He bent forward and picked a long blade of grass. "People don't trust gypsies, and the gypsies laugh at me because I collect plants like the women." He twirled the grass between his fingers. "It's what I love, though. My father wasn't around, so and I helped Mum with her healing work."

148

A lock of brown hair fell across his face as he looked into the distance. "She never asked for anything in return. When she died, I carried on for a while but..."

A pang of sorrow ran through me. "What went wrong?"

He sighed and looked up from his daisy chain. "A girl... I met her at the market. She was coughing, and I told her to wait while I fetched her a remedy. I thought she'd go, but she was still there when I returned with some elderberry syrup." A small smile touched his lips. "Ebony hair, and a smile that lit up her face. I told her she could find me at the market if she needed more. Two days later, she came back. Told me she didn't need any more because it had fixed it. I wouldn't have asked her out; she was way out of my league, but she asked me if I wanted to get a coffee, and we started seeing each other." He paused, clearly struggling with his emotions.

I wanted to help him but wasn't sure I was strong enough. "You don't have to tell me if you don't want to."

"It's okay. Her dad saw us together and forbade her to 'hang out with some gypo'."

"And she listened, just like that?"

"Daddy was rich, very rich."

"Let me guess, he threatened to disinherit her?"

He nodded. "A few days later, I met Brother Michael at the market. I guess he could tell I was lonely because he brought me here."

I smiled. "You felt accepted here."

"Yes...uh... Brother Michael said you can feel what I feel. Is it true?"

"Yes. I can do more than that. I can share it."

He smiled. "I feel... I don't know... lighter somehow. But by the looks of you, you have your own worries."

My mind went back to Karl. "I'm waiting for Scott to come. He may have news about Karl."

"He doesn't usually get here before three. The market isn't until tomorrow morning."

I looked at my watch. 01:30. "The time moves so slowly here."

"Come on. You can help me." He unfolded his legs, then stood and waited as I got up from the log.

"Help you with what?"

"I need to find some male fern."

I smiled and followed him into the trees, knowing I'd be no help at all, but glad of something to do. "How do you know if it's male?"

He sniggered. "You're funny, you know that?"

I had no idea why he was laughing at me. "What do you need it for?"

"It's not for me. It's for Callum. Ask him."

I rolled my eyes. *Why does everyone tell me to ask someone else?*

We stopped at a clearing, and I gasped. The place was magical. Dense forest gave way to daffodils and dancing light. I turned slowly around in wonder. I really wouldn't have been surprised to see fairies. "It's beautiful here."

Arin stooped and started breaking off some fern leaves. When he stood, he pointed at a small gap in the surrounding trees.

"That's the way through the forest to the outside world."

"Have you walked there?"

"Yes, but I wouldn't try it if I were you. My gypsy blood helps me to know the land. It guides me. I can leave whenever I like. I think that knowledge helps me to stay."

"I can understand that. Even though I like it here, I feel trapped."

"You'll leave when you need to."

"Have people found their way in from outside?"

"No, they can't do that." He shook his head, his eyes revealing something deeper than his words. Abruptly he turned on his heels. "Come on. I need to find Callum."

I followed him, wishing I could stay in the clearing longer. I felt safe there, and calmer. "What do you mean, people can't find their way in?"

"Sanctuary is protected. Only the invited may enter."

"Protected how?"

"That's another question for Callum."

At five to three, I stood on the cliff with Lily, waiting for Scott to arrive. My eyes were peeled along the coastline, waiting for the first glimpse of the boat. Ten minutes later, I leapt up and down with joy as it came into view. "Lily that must be him! Tell me it is!"

She squinted at the approaching boat. "Yes. I'm sure it is. Wait, Emily. Don't go hurtling down the steps; he'll be another fifteen minutes at least. I don't want you breaking your neck."

We looked towards the approaching vessel. Suddenly, she caught my arm.

I felt her love swell. "Scott. You love Scott?"

She blushed and released my arm.

"Oh, sorry, is it a secret?"

"No... it isn't anything."

I felt her love mix with pain. "Does he know how you feel?"

"No! I can't tell him." "No."

"Why not?"

She looked back at the boat, getting bigger by the second. The hand of sorrow squeezed my heart, as I guessed it was squeezing hers.

"Because, he isn't ready to hear it yet."

"Why? Is he afraid of this place?"

"He feels he could never belong here."

"Because of his sister?"

"Because he may decide to become like his sister."

Before I had the chance to ask any more questions, she turned away and started walking back to the monastery.

"Lily wait! Why don't you want to see him?"

She stopped and faced me, a smile on her lips, but sadness in her eyes. "I do."

I frowned. She wasn't making sense. "So come. I can probably tell how he feels about you if you're near him."

She looked at her feet. "I know, Emily. That's why I'm staying here. I'm not sure I want to know."

I hesitated for a moment. It seemed crazy to me, but I was too worried about Karl to argue with her.

Despite Lily's warning, I skipped down the steep steps as quickly as I could. Kicking off my shoes, I ran down the beach, then along the small wooden jetty, to meet him.

"Blimey." He called out as the boat came close, "I wasn't expecting this reception."

I hopped from one foot to the other trying to contain myself. "Any news?" I asked as he flung the rope around the mooring post.

He looked at me and rolled his eyes. "Hi, Scott. Nice to see you, Scott."

Once he'd climbed onto the jetty, I punched his arm playfully. "It's great to see you Scott, but pleeease tell me if you've heard from Karl."

"No."

"What do you mean, no?" *He's joking, or I misheard, surely?*

"I haven't heard anything."

My heart turned to lead.

"No message even?"

"No. That's good, isn't it? I'd have heard if anything bad had happened. Maybe he'll ring me tomorrow. See how you are.

I saw Tom. He's off to see family somewhere. I've no idea how much he knows, so I didn't say nothing... Hey, aren't you going to help with these pots?"

His voice had become a distant sound, like a radio, as I trudged back the beach.

K12

I felt his cool breath on my neck and waited for his hand to move across my waist, then up to my breast. A smile slowly spread across my mouth as I remembered the last time I was in his bed and my body tingled at the thought of him.

Then I woke. My eyes snapped open. This was not his bed. The tingle turned to a shudder. The dream had been sweet, but could never match reality. I jumped out of the narrow bed in my room. It was more like a cell, so basic, lacking in anything personal to me. I noticed the open window, the cause of the cool breeze – so like his breath on my skin.

I'd been looking at the stars from my window the night before, remembering the day I'd stood with Karl in the Kenwood estate. It was the first time I'd really noticed how beautiful the night was.

As I shut the window, a sob caught in my throat. Scott would come to take the clay pots to market in two days' time. I would leave with him. I was going to return to Karl, and I wouldn't listen to his arguments. We were in this together.

Later, I stood outside the lab, trying to pluck up the courage to go in and talk to Callum. I was still a little nervous of him, but I wanted to keep busy for the next couple of days until I could leave. My hand rested on the handle while I tried to think of something to say to him. *Hi, would be a good start, silly!* I chuckled to myself and gripped the handle just as it flew out of my reach and Callum stood in the open doorway.

"Are you going to hover there all day or do you want something?"

I registered mild annoyance before calm washed over it again. I felt the colour rise in my cheeks. "I was passing and wondered if I could help?"

His eyes narrowed. Maybe he was looking into my conscience.

"Did the Monks send you?"

"No. Well, they said I should talk to everyone, but I really would like to help."

He raised his eyebrows. "Do you know what it is you're offering to help with?"

"No." I peered past him at the equipment and liquids. "Are you some sort of chemist?"

"I guess that depends on your viewpoint." He stood aside and allowed me to enter. The smell was horrible and I wrinkled my nose.

He laughed, and dimples appeared in his cheeks. His face was so transformed by them, so softened, that I was left wondering why I'd been nervous.

"Most people would call me a witch."

"Really? You do spells?"

"Yes, but only for the good of Sanctuary. I use nature to protect us and replant in order to keep the balance."

"How come you said a witch, rather than a wizard?"

"Because there is no need for another name. The word *witch* comes from the word wicca for male and wicce for female. They both mean a practitioner of witchcraft."

I looked around the lab, which was actually part of the kitchen.

"Must have been a lot of mouths to feed once," Callum explained, "but now there's only a few of us, so this part has been sectioned off. Arin makes his lotions and medicines here too."

I looked in a basket of leaves and picked one up. "These are bay leaves aren't they?"

"Yes, I scatter them and sweep them up. It wards off evil."

I remembered seeing him with his broom and wondering how so many leaves had gotten indoors. I picked up a spray of tiny papery pink flowers. "What about this?"

"That's statice; it promotes peace and harmony within the group."

He was answering my questions, but I sensed he was withholding something. "Have I done something wrong?"

"What makes you say that?"

"I'm not sure. Just a feeling I had."

"Ah...Peter told me about you. Surely you can feel our friendship towards you?"

"You're all very good at feeling calm and love and peace, but I'm wondering if it's real, or just a spell."

He shrugged. "Everyone here is receptive to calm and love and peace. I just enhance it."

"I know someone who's very good at blocking feelings. He can even let some feelings through and not others, but I have learnt to tell. It leaves a void where a feeling should be. I think you're doing the same."

"I assume this person, as you call him, is Lord Ashton?" He drew his lips into a thin line.

"You don't approve of me and Karl." *At least, I know what you're hiding.* "I thought you were all supposed to be forgiving and accepting here!"

He shrugged. "Only for those who want to be forgiven and accepted."

"You shouldn't assume you know him."

"I don't think that you should either."

I felt anger well up inside me, even though I didn't really blame him for the way he felt about Karl. I knew the rest of the world would never see the same Karl that I saw. I turned to leave before I said something I might regret.

"Wait, Emily. I don't mean to upset you. I just don't understand how you could waste your gift."

I turned back to him, confused. "What gift?"

"The gift of empathy, real empathy. There are fewer Empaths in the world than witches and vampires. Actually, you're the first one I've met."

I stared at him, trying to take in his words. "An Empath? Is that what I am?"

"Yes, you have the power to share people's feelings and to change them. Just think of all the hardship there is in this world, all the innocent people suffering. You could relieve some of their pain. You could have chosen to work in a hospital, or become a missionary, but you chose to become a cleaner for a vampire! Do you see why I think it's a waste?"

I felt his frustration.

Have I been selfish? I realised, with a pang of guilt, I had. I hadn't given a thought to how much good I could do, by sharing people's pain. I'd only thought about the hurt it caused me. Except with Karl, that is. *Haven't I always known I was needed at Kenwood?*

I crossed my arms and glared at him defensively. "But you don't understand. I didn't realise. I'm not always sure if I'm getting it right, or feeling what I want to feel."

"Trust your instincts. You do know, but you doubt yourself."

"I didn't know I could make a difference to someone's life. Not until I met Karl. I believe I can help him. But you need to realise, he's helped me too. I'm starting to believe in myself. If I can find love in the most battered of hearts, surely it must count for something?"

Callum sighed and nodded; his calm had returned. "I know you could do so much more, but maybe you will. I'm sorry, I forget you're only young and it's not for me to judge you. I know Michael and Peter would certainly agree that it's important to help those who sin, as much as those who don't." His eyes bored into mine. "I suppose it's to your credit

157

that you find good in the darkest of places. I just hope it doesn't get you killed."

"So do I." I grinned at him. "Luckily, I know a witch who can do protection spells."

He grinned back. "Do you still want to help? I hope we can be friends."

He held out his hand and I shook it.

"Sure, what do you want me to do?"

Later, we burnt hyssop in iron bowls around the grounds while Callum chanted something strange in Latin.

"Is this another protection spell?" I asked.

"Yes. It calls on the power of the dragons."

"The what? Don't tell me dragons are real too."

Callum chuckled. "Not anymore, although I believe they walked with the dinosaurs. Rumour has it that there may still be eggs underground, just waiting for a climate change so the dragons can return."

I laughed. "I think that's a stretch of the imagination too far."

He turned to me, eyebrows raised. "Says the girl whose boyfriend is a vampire."

My stomach rumbled as I made my way to the dining room for dinner. Having enjoyed the time spent with Callum, I decided I would make more effort to speak to Moira.

Moira kept herself at a distance and yet she bothered me. It was the way she looked at me. Her strong jaw and long nose were slightly masculine but softened by her full mouth. Her hair was platinum blonde and layered to her shoulders. But it was her large, almond-shaped eyes that disturbed me. Their icy blue gaze seemed so intelligent, so knowing. Did she know something about me? Or Karl? *Is that why she avoids me?*

Having decided to approach her after dinner, I was disappointed she wasn't there. I thought, at first, she may just be late, but after I'd finished eating, she was still absent. Arin sat down next to me and I asked him if Moira was okay.

"Yeah, sure. I mean, she's a bit under the weather." His eyes darted to Michael as he spoke, and he picked at his nails.

Even if I hadn't felt his anxiety, I would have known he was lying. It was the first lie I'd detected since I arrived at Sanctuary, and it intrigued me.

I went to the kitchen to take my turn at washing up. As the water whirled around, so did my mind. *What is Karl doing right now? Is he thinking of me?*

"Don't take it personally."

I jumped at the voice behind me. Tyler stood, arms loaded with dishes, then plonked them down beside me.

"What?" I had no idea what he meant.

He blew an auburn lock of hair away from his eye. "Back there," he replied, nodding to the dining room, "about Moira. Michael thinks we should leave it to her to tell you about herself."

"She doesn't seem keen. I don't understand what I've done, but she's definitely avoided me. I thought you were too."

"I'm sure you didn't mind too much. I'm the boring one after all."

I frowned at him. I'd been less interested in getting to know him, it was true. He never seemed to join in with the others. He always seemed part of the surroundings, until now.

I narrowed my eyes with suspicion. "Did Michael send you to talk to me?"

He picked up a tea towel and began drying the dishes. "No. I just thought I should tell you not to bother going to Moira's room to see how she is. She won't answer."

"How do you know she won't?"

"Because she isn't in it. Just wait, I think she'll talk to you in her own time."

How did he know what I'd been planning to do? I tried to remember if I had said it out loud, but I didn't think so.

"No, you didn't say it out loud."

My mouth dropped open as I remembered my conversation with Lily. I'd asked her if she could read my mind and she'd said: "No, not me".

"You can read my mind!"

"Yes."

"Everything?"

"Yes. Don't worry; I'll forgive you for thinking I was too boring to talk to."

"That's not true, I ..." I realised there was no point trying to be polite when he knew my every thought. "I guess I shouldn't have judged a book by its cover, but you don't exactly seek attention."

Close up, I noticed the pale skin of his face was scattered with freckles, and his hazel eyes glittered mischievously. *He's anything but boring.*

"You must know what it's like to get no peace from other people, only with you, it's feelings, with me it's thoughts."

"It must be noisy."

"It's hell. Not as bad here, though. I come for a rest when I can't cope with the outside world. It's been a bit noisier lately."

"How come?"

He laughed and I realised what he meant.

"You mean because I arrived?"

He glanced at me sideways from the plate he was wiping. "You do have a lot on your mind."

I tried to remember what else I might have thought about when he was near. I must have thought about Karl and how worried I was. What else? Mostly Karl. I'd probably thought about Karl and me together. Had I thought about us having sex? Oh God!

I blushed to the roots as I realised he was hearing me even now.

Tyler laughed again. "I wouldn't feel too embarrassed. It isn't the first time I've heard things I'm not meant to, especially living with two gay monks!"

I thought about this for a second and laughed myself. I knew only too well that he couldn't help knowing more about people than they wanted him to.

"I knew you would understand." He smiled at me and I could feel the warmth of his happiness.

"Yes, it's much calmer here and I don't struggle with people's feelings the way I do outside. It would be nice to switch it off sometimes."

"It's good to meet someone with a similar affliction." He stopped and turned to me, eyes twinkling.

At last, someone who gets it. "Callum calls it a gift. He was quite cross with me for wasting it."

"Callum wants to save the world, which is very noble, but I just want to survive one day at a time. At least, you can make a difference. You can take on some of their feelings. Share the load. I can't influence people's thoughts, just listen to them."

"By sharing the load, you mean I can suffer with them. Great."

"Sorry, guess I hadn't thought. Must hurt like hell sometimes."

I nodded. I wished more people had his insight. "So, what's Moira's problem with me?"

He turned back to the dishes, suddenly keen to put them away. His head disappeared in a cupboard. "She doesn't have a problem with you," he replied. "It's your, shall we say, acquaintances?"

"Vampires? Or Karl in particular?"

His head popped out from the cupboard. "You really must let her decide whether to tell you. She'll be better in a couple of days."

"How do you know that?"

"Has anyone told you, you ask too many questions?"

"Yes, Karl has, several times, but I still ask them."

"She often has spells of illness like this and she likes to go and be on her own somewhere. We don't disturb her and she's always better after a couple of days. Now, that's all I'm saying on the matter."

We finished the washing up and walked towards the common room, where we could read and talk in the evenings. There was no television, but we had cards and some board games. I was surprised that I enjoyed the evenings there. "I don't recall ever seeing you in the common room. Are you joining us tonight?"

"I might, if you promise to keep your thoughts pure."

I blushed again and replied, "I will if you keep your feelings uncomplicated."

"Okay, it's a deal." He stopped and turned to me. "There is something I need to tell you first."

"Oh?" I was uneasy now, as he looked serious.

"I know you don't plan to be here in a couple of days, and you think you'll never get chance to speak to Moira anyway."

I nodded in agreement.

"I advise you to stay longer." His eyes were locked on mine, his voice urgent. "You may put your boyfriend in danger if you leave."

"What do you mean? How could I endanger him?"

"You may not thank me for interfering and telling you this, but I know how much you respect honesty. Lily didn't tell you everything. She knows I must know the truth, but the others don't."

"Truth about what?"

"Her visions. She's seen something; she's seen an explosion at Kenwood Manor."

My chest tightened. "No! I can't believe she would lie to me. She said everything was okay. You mean he could have been harmed already and I wouldn't know. I must get out of here. I need to find out."

"Wait. You don't understand. She was telling the truth when she said nothing had happened yet. Lily sees things in the future as well as the present. She knows it hasn't happened yet because...well, in the vision, you are there when the explosion happens. I'm sorry, Emily. I don't know if you survive it or who else is involved. I can't see her visions. I have only read her concerns about you and Scott."

"So as long as I'm here...?"

"The manor is safe. I believe futures can be changed, Emily, but you can't just go rushing in. You should talk to Lily, and we'll try and think of something to help you."

"We?"

"You're one of us now."

"The house, how bad is the explosion?" I held my breath, waiting for a response that didn't come. "Tyler, please tell me."

He rested his hands on my shoulders and spoke very quietly. "If I read her thoughts correctly, there won't be much left."

K13

I dashed into the common room. Lily wasn't there. I tore up the stairs to her room and banged on the door.

Tyler came rushing after me. "Emily, calm down. She was only worried about upsetting you."

"Well, guess what, I *am* upset!" My whole body trembled. *How dare they expect me to make friends with everyone when they hide the truth from me whenever they like.*

"I'm not hiding anything from you." Tyler reached out to comfort me, but I wasn't in the mood to be reasonable.

"Stop reading my bloody mind, will you!" My vision blurred as my eyes filled with tears.

"You know I can't help it."

I did know, and I knew he was the one person who had been completely honest.

I banged the door again; there was no answer from Lily, and the anger went out of me, to be replaced by anguish and loneliness. "You don't understand; none of you do. I've already found my sanctuary: Kenwood Manor. I can't just stand by while it's destroyed." The tears began to fall. I could feel Tyler's awkwardness, but I couldn't help it.

He squeezed my shoulder. "Sanctuary isn't a physical place, Emily. It's a feeling or a place you can go in your mind. If you've found it once, you can find it again, no matter what happens to the Manor."

I glared at him. "You come here, to a physical place, for your sanctuary."

"Yes, but it's the people that make it feel like sanctuary, not the walls."

I looked down the corridor. Each door had the occupants name on it, carefully carved out of wood by Arin. I turned back to the door I was standing next to and touched the plaque with Lily's name. "And if the people are destroyed? What if Karl is destroyed? I know you probably don't even think of him as a person, but I do, and I don't think I could find any sanctuary without him. I don't want to."

I heard humming behind me and turned as Lily came along the corridor, carrying a small book.

I folded my arms across my chest. "Why didn't you tell me?"

She stopped humming, eyes wide. "Tell you what, Emily?"

"About your vision."

She looked at Tyler and frowned.

He held up his hands. "She was planning to go back. I had to tell her."

Lily looked back to me with sadness in her eyes. "There isn't much to tell. I don't know who else was there, or whether anyone gets hurt."

I sighed and relaxed my arms. "Tell me exactly what you saw. Please, Lily."

"Okay, but you have to understand, it isn't like watching a movie. It comes in short flashes which are hard to understand and can be easily misinterpreted."

"Go on."

"I saw you running across grass. I think there must be an explosion because bits of concrete and glass are flying through the air, and there are dark shapes moving fast. I saw a house, or rather a ruin. But I don't know *which* house. It could be anywhere."

I clenched my fists in frustration. "Can't you try and see it again?"

"I'm sorry. It doesn't work that way."

"What about the house? What colour was it? How big?"

She glanced sideways at Tyler, then back at me. "I couldn't tell. It was just rubble."

Too overwhelmed to say more, I ran to my room. There, the pain I'd been holding in came out in a cry. For once, I wanted to be alone. My mind whirled with questions. *What should I do? How can I warn Karl? What if something happens to Kenwood Manor?*

Unable to think of an answer, I lay on my bed. Sleep took a long time coming, and when it did, I dreamt I was lost, unable to find my home or my lover.

The next morning, I was about to accompany Arin down to the cliff with the pottery for market, when I had an idea.

"You carry on, Arin. I'll be down in a minute."

He sauntered off, and I went to look for Tyler. I found him milking a tethered goat in the small paddock to the rear of the monastery. He was sitting on a small stool, expertly sending small streams of creamy milk into a metal bucket, whilst several other goats skipped around merrily.

I leant on the gate to the paddock. "Hi, Tyler. Just wondering if you could come to the beach and help us with the pottery."

He looked up and paused his milking. "I thought Arin was going with you."

"He is, but there are quite a few supplies coming in on the boat today, so we could do with an extra pair of hands." *And I know you can read the real reason I want you to come, so why are you asking?*

He laughed. "Cheeky woman!"

Noticing his distraction, the brown and white goat he was milking, kicked its back legs and bounded forward. Realising she couldn't get far, she ran around the post she was tied to, bleating and kicking up her heals. Tyler stood up and watched with hands on hips. "Bloody goats, you can't take your eyes off them for a moment." Despite his words, he was laughing.

"Sorry, Tyler. It's my fault for distracting you."

He turned and shook his head. "No. They're always getting the better of me. At least, she didn't kick the milk over this time." He released the goat and she skipped away with her friends. Picking up the bucket, he wandered over to the gate.

"So, will you come?"

"I don't know. I don't usually read minds deliberately."

"Even when it's life or death? I just want you to tell me if Scott tells the truth when I ask him how things are at home. I know I will feel his guilt if he lies, but I won't know what the truth is."

He rolled his eyes and sighed. "Okay, just this once."

I stood back, allowing him through the gate.

"Thanks. If you happen to find out what he thinks of Lily while you're there, let me know."

He looked sideways at me. "Hmm. Is that a life or death situation as well?"

I grinned. "No. It's love, which is just as important."

He shook his head, but as we walked past the stone outbuildings that housed the animals at night, he put his bucket in the shade and followed me towards the cliff-top.

A pulley system had been fixed to the edge of the cliff, which allowed us to lower the pottery without carrying them down the steps. When we arrived at the top, we could see that Arin and Scott had already got the pots safely onto the beach, and were loading the boat.

I turned to Tyler. "Oops, I won't be popular now! I should have been helping."

"He smiled. I'm sure they'll forgive you, and we can offer to take the supplies up."

We made our way towards the steep steps, the salty smell filling my lungs. I squinted in the sunlight as I looked at Tyler. "The pots are beautiful. Do the monks make all of them?"

"Yes, they sell well in the market. The money pays for supplies and we give Scott a small amount for his trouble."

We descended the steps in silence, concentrating on our footing. The only sounds I heard were the waves crashing against the shore and the seagulls.

Once on the beach, we hurried to where Scott was lifting beautiful rustic pots from a big, flat-bed trolley. "Hi Scott, how is everything back at Kenwood?"

He glanced at Tyler then back at me. "Fine, there hasn't been any trouble. Lord Ashton wants you to stay away a bit longer to be on the safe side. Benedikte will be back soon. He plans to hunt the hunters. They won't stand a chance."

I picture of Daniel in the car park flashed through my mind. "I wouldn't underestimate them."

"Benedikte won't be alone. He has loads of loyal followers, vampires and humans. He's seriously hard core. If you'd met him, you'd know what I mean. He talks all polite, but if you cross him." He made a slicing gesture across his throat.

"As long as he leads them away from the manor. I hope Karl doesn't get involved."

His raised eyebrows told me what I feared. "At least, you'll be free to go back when it's over."

"But my parents must be wondering where I am. So must my friends. If only I could phone them, but there's never any signal here."

He rummaged in one of the bags and produced some postcards. "Here, fill these in," he said. "I'll take them back to post."

I recognised the pictures of Blackpool Tower, many miles away, and suppressed a sigh. *More lies to my friends and family.* "Thanks. It's really kind of you."

"Lord Ashton told me to get them. Thought you'd want to let people know you're okay."

"And he's really alright?"

"Yes. As I said." He handed me a white envelope. "Here, he asked me to give you this."

My fingers trembled as I took the letter and slipped it into my pocket. I knew his smile was fake, and I had to know more. "If everything's okay, why are you worrying?"

His eyes darted between me and Tyler. I looked to Tyler for help.

Tyler's attention shifted to Scott. "He's telling the truth about Lord Ashton not being hurt."

"See," snapped Scott.

Tyler kept his eyes fixed on Scott. "But he's hiding something."

Scott's nostrils flared. "Damn it, Tyler, you'll get me killed!"

A wave of male anger mixed with fear pierced me, boring its way to the pit of my stomach. As I pushed off the force of emotions, I could see Tyler was trying to read Scott.

Scott shook his head, backing away. "Tyler, please! You don't know him. He'll kill me if I disobey."

Scott backed away around the side of the boat. Arin, who'd been busy wrapping the pots in bubble wrap and stowing them safely away, stood up and smiled.

Tyler raised a hand to Arin, then turned back to Scott. "Don't worry, you haven't told us anything. It looks like Arin has finished loading your boat. You should go now."

I was frantic. "He isn't going anywhere until he tells me!"

"Look at him, Emily. He's too scared to tell us anything. Let him go. Lord Ashton is safe, I promise."

I shook my head in disbelief.

Scott grabbed the mooring rope and leapt aboard his boat. "I'm sorry, Emily, but it really isn't anything you need to worry about. He just thinks you'll worry unnecessarily."

Arin jumped down onto the jetty and Scott passed a large crate to him. Arin put it on the jetty then reached for the second one. Once the supplies were off the boat, Scott disappeared into the cabin, and the out-board motor kicked into life.

"Are you two coming?" Arin asked, as we watched the boat pull away.

"In a minute. You go on, me and Tyler will take the supplies up."

"Cool." He sauntered back across the beach.

I turned to Tyler. "You know, don't you? You know what he was hiding."

He didn't speak for a moment, and then he turned to me. "Yes. I thought Scott would be happier if he thought he'd kept his thoughts to himself. He tried to block me by thinking about what Lord Ashton would do to him. You don't seem to realise how scared he is of him, Emily. You don't even realise he has reason to be."

"So, you're not going to tell me?"

"I don't know."

I looked down at the postcards in my hand. "I didn't fill them in"

"Don't worry. Arin can get them to a post-box for you."

We lifted the crates onto the trolley and wheeled them slowly across the sand. As we transferred the supplies to the pulley, Tyler turned to me. "By the way, he does like her. Scott I mean; he likes Lily."

I stood back, surprised. "How do you know? We never mentioned her."

"He was looking out for her. Disappointed she wasn't with us."

"Good. I hope they get together one day."

We walked towards the steps. "So, have you decided? Will you tell me?" I stood waiting for Tyler's decision.

He looked down at his feet and pushed a shell across the sand with the toe of his shoe. Finally, he looked at me. "Do you know a vampire called Ana?"

I winced, as pain struck my heart. "Yes."

"She's there, in the Manor."

I fled from Tyler and headed up the steps. I took them two at a time with no thought for my safety. At the top, breathless, I headed for the monastery. Why would he have let her back there? Had I been naive in believing it was over between them? Perhaps he'd been sleeping with her all along? I was sure Scott felt there was no need for me to worry, but what did he know? Karl was hardly likely to tell him about his sex life.

At the big oak door to the monastery, I stopped and took a deep breath of cool sea air. *Get a grip girl! What you felt from Karl was real. He loves you.*

When I reached my room, I hurled myself on the bed, pulled the envelope from my pocket and tore it open.

> *Everything is going to be fine, Emily.*
> *Tom is staying with family and so is Ned.*
> *I have gathered as many vampires together as I can, and Benedikte is on his way.*
> *It will soon be over, and we will be together again.*
> *I miss you*
>
> *K xxxx*

I read the letter twice, then the page blurred as tears rolled down my face. *Oh, Karl, I miss you so much. If only I could see you, or at least talk to you. I can't bear to be so far away from you.*

Tyler knocked on my door, and then the Brothers. I asked them all to leave me alone.

I ran out of tears by midnight.

Pulling myself together, I read the letter again and, despite everything, I smiled. Perhaps Karl *was* just gathering as many vampires as he could for a battle, but someone must have talked to Daniel about Karl and me. Ana was the only person who had seen us together. Had she betrayed him? I thought about the explosion Lily had seen. If it was Kenwood, someone would have put the explosives inside the Manor grounds. Someone Karl trusted enough to let through the security. I would have to contact Karl somehow and warn him.

I stood, looking out of the window. The yard below was bathed in the light of the full moon and I leant forward to let it illuminate my skin. There was a faint noise from below me and I leant out even further. Across the courtyard, the main door opened and Arin stepped outside. I pulled my head back a bit so he wouldn't notice me. He carried something in a big tray, something dark and wet looking. Even in the moonlight, it was hard to see exactly what he carried, but it looked like meat, large chunks of dark meat.

Where on earth is he taking that in the middle of the night? He crossed the courtyard and disappeared through the main gate.

The next morning, I decided I would leave after breakfast, but first, I had to persuade Arin to show me the way. I looked at my suitcase, it was small, but there was no way I could drag it miles through the woods. I went to Lily's room and asked her if she had a holdall I could borrow.

"I've got a backpack, but I wish you'd rethink this. Please, stay."

"I can't. I need to warn him."

She nodded. "I understand, but I'll miss you."

I hugged her. She smelt of jasmine. "I'll miss you too." I turned to go, then remembered something. "You should tell Scott how you feel. He likes you."

A ray of hope soared from her to me, like a tiny bird. "Are you sure?"

I nodded. "I took Tyler to the beach with me. Life's too short not to be with the one you love, Lily.

At breakfast, I reassured the Monks and Tyler that I was feeling much better. I felt their approval as I polished off a fried breakfast. But it was soon replaced by anxiety when I told them my plans.

Brother Peter laid his hand gently over mine. "We'll be here whenever you need us, Emily."

I nodded, smiling at my new friends. "Thanks, all of you, but I need to get going."

My head was full of finding Arin and enlisting his help. I dashed around the grounds and finally found him in the herb garden. He was on his knees, pulling weeds. When I explained my plans, he stood and fixed his eyes on mine.

"Are you mad? You're safe here and among friends. Why do you want to go running towards trouble?"

"You know why."

"And you think he'll be pleased that you're leaving here and putting yourself in danger?"

"No. But I doubt he'll be surprised either. I have to warn him. Maybe I'm a fool and he only wants me out of the way so he can see Ana, but why would he bother to lie? Surely, he would just kill me or ignore me if he didn't care. I need to see him Arin. Please help me."

He wiped his filthy hands in his jumper. "Sorry, Emily. I can't help you. I don't want to piss him off, and I happen to think he's right to have sent you here"

I could feel the truth in his words. But they didn't satisfy me.

"Like I said, we're your friends."

"Friends who keep secrets from me."

"If this is about Moira, you can wait until later and talk to her. She'll be back soon."

"How do you know?"

"I just do."

"Where were you going with a large tray of meat last night?"

His eyes widened in surprise.

"I saw you out of my window. The full moon lit up the whole courtyard."

"I took it to feed the eagles that live on the cliff."

"At midnight?"

"They hunt at night; I couldn't sleep."

I knew he was lying and I think he knew it. I also had a feeling I'd missed something. I looked at him for a moment and then gave up. Getting out was my priority.

I shrugged. "Okay, but I do need your help. All I'm asking is for you to take me to the edge of the woods and point me to a road. I have my mobile back and some money. As soon as I get a signal, I can use the map app on the phone and get a bus or cab. Karl doesn't need to know how I got out. I'll warn him not to trust Ana or let her have free access to the house, then I'll come back."

His fear stabbed at my chest.

"I won't go into the grounds of the house, I promise, Arin, so you needn't worry. I'll send Karl a message to meet me somewhere else."

An hour later, I said my goodbyes and met Arin in the courtyard. He'd filled a bag with bread rolls, cheese and a bottle of lemonade.

"Wait!" It was Callum, running towards me with something in his hand. "I heard you were leaving and wanted to give you something to protect yourself."

I took the tiny white bag, hanging from a leather string "Thank you. What is it?"

"Angelica root, also known as Holy Ghost root. It acts as a powerful guardian and healer. You should wear it."

I smiled and hung it around my neck, aware I had a tear in my eye. "Thanks... thanks for everything."

As I walked towards the wood with Arin, I was surprised to see Moira emerging, looking tired and dishevelled. Her platinum-blonde hair hung in rattails and her blue eyes blinked in the light.

"Hi," I said, as she glanced from me to Arin.

"Emily is leaving us," Arin explained. "For a while at least."

"Oh, I'm sorry."

And she was; I could feel it. "I'm sorry I didn't get to know you, Moira. Maybe another time."

She smiled and nodded. "Maybe."

And I noticed that her eyes were a lot like Karl's. I don't mean the colour or even the shape, but like him, her eyes seemed to have seen more years than they should have.

I wasn't as fit as I thought, and my trainers weren't as comfy as I expected. Rain began and continued on and on, getting heavier, until I could hardly see in front of me. Tree after tree all looked the same to me. No track to follow, only Arin, who seemed to follow nothing but his nose. I began to slide on mud and then I fell, cutting my forehead on a rock.

"We have to stop, Emily. The storm is getting worse and you have blood running into your eyes."

With little fight left in me, I shook my head. "Come on, I know where there's shelter." He dragged me by the arm until we reached a wooden hut. "I think it's been used by hunters."

It was small, but it was shelter and I was exhausted.

"Emily! Are you okay? How many fingers am I holding up?"

"Three and I'm fine; I just need a rest."

But after two nights of little sleep, worrying about the man and the house I loved, my body gave in.

I slept and dreamt of a wolf, a wolf with white fur and icy-blue eyes.

K14

I awoke with a sick feeling in my stomach and a throbbing pain in my skull. Arin had one hand on my forehead, a wet cloth in his other. "You have a fever. We'll have to stay put."

I groaned in protest and tried to get up but my legs gave way beneath me. He shook his head. I'm popping out to find some plants to cool your fever. I know some grow nearby."

I was so desperate to find Karl, but the heat overtook my senses and I tossed and turned in and out of sleep. Arin returned with a fistful of herbs. I took whatever he gave me and hoped it would work quickly.

When I woke again, I felt cooler. Sitting up, I stretched my legs, then gradually tested my weight on them. They were strong enough to hold me though my blistered feet hurt. Keen to keep moving, I slipped on my trainers and stepped outside of the wooden hut to find Arin. He was sitting beside a fire, cooking something on a stick. My stomach grumbled loudly.

"Hi, Arin. Thanks for taking care of me."

He looked around and smiled. "No problem. I bet you're hungry."

I was, but I wasn't sure about the strange looking things on sticks. "Er… yes. What are those?"

"Squirrel."

"Eew, I think I'll pass."

"You need to eat something if you want to move on tomorrow."

My pulse began throbbing in my head. "Tomorrow? Can't we keep going today? I'm much better now. I'll even eat squirrel." I'd crossed the space between us, trying not to show my wincing, at every painful step.

Arin shook his head and pointed at the sun sinking slowly in the sky. "Too late in the day. There won't be any more shelter between here and the road, and there's not enough time to make it before dark."

I sighed and slumped down beside him on a log. "Seriously. I've been asleep all day?"

He raised his eyebrows and passed me a squirrel on a stick. "It wasn't last night you hurt your head, Emily. It was the night before."

The horror of it hit me like a punch to the gut. "What! Anything could have happened by now. I need to get out of here." I leapt up, waving my squirrel in the air. Then collapsed again as pain throbbed through my head, and my feet screamed in pain.

Arin caught hold of my arm, his eyes locking onto mine. "You're not going anywhere today. You need to eat and rest. Karl can look after himself."

My lip quivered as I held my tears in check. "But…"

"No buts. Eat your squirrel."

I looked down at the meat, my mind a whirl. Anxiety for Karl mixed with guilt that I'd put Arin to so much trouble. I picked at the meat and put some in my mouth. It wasn't too bad. Peering up through my lashes, I noticed Arin smiling. His friendship warmed me.

"I must have looked quite a sight waving that stick around and wailing like a banshee." I gave him a weak smile.

He chuckled. "At least, you provided me with some evening entertainment."

The next chunk of meat flew from my hand and hit him on the arm.

"Hey, don't waste good squirrel." He pulled a face that was meant to look cross, but made me laugh.

When my laughing subsided, I realised the weight in my chest seemed lighter. I was still worried, but Arin was right.

Karl was no fool. He could look after himself. Maybe I wanted him to need me more than he actually did. I was the one who needed looking after. A pang of guilt shot through me.

"I'm sorry Arin. I've been selfish, again."

"Whatdya mean?"

"Dragging you out here."

He shrugged. "I like it out here. This is what I was born for, nature and healing."

"Well, I appreciate it, thanks."

"No problem. And I don't think you're selfish. You love him. I get it."

I smiled, relieved. He did look at home by the fire, and I was lucky to have him as a guide. That night I slept more soundly.

The next day, we rose early and started walking. Arin with long agile strides; me more gingerly on blistered feet. Eventually, I stumbled from the forest on sore feet and aching legs.

The first thing I did was check my mobile signal. "Three bars, Arin!" My pain momentarily forgotten, I jumped into the air, then cursed as my tortured feet shot messages to my brain. Almost delirious with the thought of seeing Karl, I dialled Kenwood manor. My spirits soared, hearing Tom's voice, then sank as I realised it was an answering machine – something new.

"You'd better ring Scott, Emily. You could do with a wash before you see Karl."

"You don't smell so good yourself."

"No offence, but for God sake don't tell him I had anything to do with you getting in that state."

I scowled, then smiled, remembering how kind Arin had been. "Will you come with us? I'm sure Scott will take you back by boat."

"No. I'm fine to go back through the forest."

"You can go now if you want. I'll be fine. And thanks. For everything."

He gave a shy smile. "I'll stay till Scott meets you. And you're welcome."

When Scott arrived, he scowled at both of us. "Have you lost your mind, Arin? Look at her! He'll skin me alive."

"I am standing here, Scott," I cut in, "I'll be fine once I've had a bath and some food. Then you can take me to Karl."

He looked exasperated, but nodded towards the car and told me to get in. I said goodbye to Arin and he waved us off.

When we got to Scott's house, I bathed as quickly as possible, but had no clean clothes, so Scott lent me a long jumper, which I fashioned into a dress using a belt. Everything seemed to take too long. My fingers fumbled at the buckle, my legs trembled with excitement, and I kept dropping the comb Scott lent me. I just wanted to see Karl. Nothing else mattered. Finally ready, I rushed downstairs and found Scott in the kitchen.

"Emily, I've been thinking. I'm not driving you to Kenwood." He took a step back as he said it. Had he anticipated my fury?

"You what? Why not?" My hands were clenched into tight fists; my heart was pounding. Anger fuelled my blood like nitroglycerine in a car engine.

"Calm down. I'll take him a note. It's safer that way. He'll go nuts if I just turn up with you. Nuts at me!"

Damn, he was right.

Not to agree would be selfish, and I was trying really hard not to be selfish. I kicked the door post. "Shit!" Pity, I'd forgotten about my sore feet.

I sat down and tried to still my shaking hand long enough to write a note. In it, I explained about Lily's vision, and my concern about him trusting Ana. I also made it clear that Scott hadn't had anything to do with me leaving Sanctuary, nor had he told me anything about Ana, but I'd known he was hiding something (I thought it better not to mention Tyler). I wanted to beg him to come, but I still had some pride. I ended with I love yous and kisses, hoping he'd come anyway.

As Scott took the note, anxiety pinched my heart – was it Scott's or mine? Either way, I was sorry I'd had to involve him.

Scott was gone for several hours. If the carpet hadn't been thin before, it certainly was after all the pacing I did. Thoughts of Karl, folding me into his arms, mixed with thoughts of him being in danger, or angry with me. My insides were a cauldron of bubbling heat.

I cleaned the kitchen. It was better than pacing and mildly therapeutic.

About four o'clock, Scott came rushing through the door with panic pouring from him like an erupting volcano.

My own fear rose to match his. "What is it? Scott, for God's sake, stand still and tell me."

"He's coming here! He doesn't want you to go to the house, but he said he wants to see you, so he's coming here! Shit, shit, shit!"

I was instantly elated and anxious at the same time.

"What's the problem with him coming here?"

"The place is a state; he'll be mad that I've let you stay in this filth."

"Scott, have you actually looked around you yet?"

He stopped and took in the gleaming sink and kettle and the tidy surfaces. His feelings calmed and his eyes were wide with amazement.

"Wow, even the cooker looks clean. This must have taken ages."

"Not really, I'm used to cleaning the Manor, remember." My emotions began swirling again at the thought of home. "He's really coming here? You're sure? What time?"

"He just said this evening. I better tidy the rest of the place."

"Okay, but calm down. I'll help." His anxiety still met me in waves.

"Why would he want to hurt you when you're so useful? He would respect you more if you were less scared of him."

"Who told you that? Him?"

"He was saying it about Tom, but I think it applies to everyone. He seems to hate people simpering around him. I'm not saying he would tolerate people being disrespectful, but he would respect people standing up to him more."

"And you have met other living human beings who would vouch for that?"

I was silent.

"Thought not."

At seven 'o'clock, there was a rap at the door, and Scott rushed to answer it. My emotions were in turmoil. I wanted to see Karl, to hold him, but I was afraid he'd be angry with me for not doing as he said. Words ran through my head, things I wanted to say, but as he stepped past Scott, his gaze stilled my lips and quickened my heart.

"Scott, disappear for a while." As he spoke, his green eyes remained fixed on mine. My legs weakened. The door clicked shut behind Scott.

"Emily."

The distance between us vanished in a heartbeat, and I lost myself in his kiss. Giddy with desire, I melted against him, not wanting to think, just feel. But my mind was cruel. Thoughts of danger dragged me back to reality. I tore myself away. "Karl, I need to talk to you."

As I spoke, he raised his fingers to my forehead and frowned. "What happened to your head?"

"It's nothing, honestly. You know how clumsy I can be. I thought you'd be angry with me for coming here."

"I should be furious, but I'm just glad to see you." He gently kissed my forehead, and I felt the coolness of his lips against my skin. His mouth moved to my lips, and the kisses became more urgent. He pulled me into the living room and onto his lap on the sofa. I tried to return his passion, but images of Ana's face kept flashing across my mind.

He stopped and looked at me. "What's wrong?"

I pulled back from him. "Ana. I told you what I thought in my letter. Is she at Kenwood Manor?"

"Yes, but so are several other vampires." He took my face in his hands. "I don't blame you for not trusting her; I don't completely trust her either. But I don't believe she would betray me. Now, can we stop talking about her?" His lusty eyes locked onto mine, sending a thrill through my body.

I covered his hands with my own. "But I'm worried about you. Who else could have told Daniel about us?"

He sighed and pulled me to his chest, kissing my hair. "I don't know; perhaps he'd been watching the house for ages."

"And the explosion that Lily saw?"

"You said in the letter she didn't see much. You don't know if anyone was hurt, or if the house was definitely Kenwood Manor."

"Where else would it be?"

"Have you any evidence that her visions are even reliable?"

I shook my head, coiling my arms around his neck. "Just promise me you'll keep an eye out for anyone carrying explosives."

"I promise. Shhh. Stop talking, so I can make love to you."

I grinned and moved so I sat astride him. "Yes, my Lord, your wish is my command."

"Good, then I wish you were naked."

We tugged off each other's clothes, devouring each other with kisses as we went. When he pulled back my hair and kissed my neck, shivers of pleasure pulsed through my body; so dangerous, but divine. Sat astride him, I lowered myself, inch by delicious inch. His heart beat slow but strong under the palm of my hand; his tongue explored my ear.

He moaned, as I moved slowly against him. Sliding his hands down my back to my hips, he grasped me tightly, and guided me faster, as he entered deeper.

The heat pulsing through my body exploded, sending a rush of pure pleasure through every nerve. I held onto him tightly as I felt him shudder beneath me. Then we were still, apart from the heavy rise and fall of our chests.

Later, I lay in his arms as he twirled my hair in his fingers.

"I love your hair, it's like sunshine, but I can hold it in my hands."

I smiled. "Thanks, but I hope you love all of me."

He chuckled and kissed my shoulder. "You know I do."

"Do you have to go tonight? Can't you stay here with me?" The thought of us parting again wrenched at my heart.

"Sorry, no. Benedikte will be here in a couple of days. I can't just leave him to fight the battle without me.

"Why's he taking so long?"

"He has to travel by night from Romania. It will be over soon, I promise. If they don't attack us, we'll attack them. Prof found out where their headquarters are. They have no idea that we know."

"And Tom?"

"Staying in Southampton with a cousin. He'll be fine; he's taken his horses with him." He began twirling my hair again, then held it against his cheek. "We'll all be fine. When you get back, we'll tell Tom about us. You should be the lady of the manor."

"Being with you is enough. And Toby's portrait is safe in my room, with the book you gave me. I want to bring them home. I miss you so much."

"I miss you too." He hugged me tightly to him, then looked up suddenly. "I can hear Scott coming; we should get dressed."

I reluctantly untangled my body from his and pulled on Scott's jumper.

"I brought you some spare clothes, they're in the car." He stopped as he zipped up his jeans, grinning at me. "You look adorable in that jumper."

I shot him a mock scowl. "Don't joke."

"I'm not. I never joke; don't know how."

The front door clicked, followed by sounds of Scott moving around in the kitchen.

"I should be getting back, Emily. Go back to Sanctuary with Scott tomorrow. I assume they treat you well?"

I nodded. "I like it there, but it isn't home." I watched him pull on his t-shirt. "I meant to ask. How do you know about sanctuary?"

He dropped a kiss on my head. "I've known it existed for ages. Scott gave me details."

"What details?"

"Enough to know they'd look after you. Now, I must go, but I'll let you know when it's safe to come home."

"Don't worry, I'll wait."

He hugged me, then turned, shoving the kitchen door open. It flew back, hitting the wall and cracking the frame; plaster fell from the wall. "Damn, forget my strength sometimes." Scott's face turned pale, his body quivering. He watched Karl march across the room and out of the front door.

For a moment, I was distracted by Scott's distress, but it was only a door. Karl hadn't meant any harm. My anxiety rose. When would I see him again? I didn't want to go back to Sanctuary. It was too isolated. I'd need Scott's help to stay, but why would he risk it? I should do something for him. Thinking quickly, I ran after Karl. He was heading back with a bag.

"Here, your spare clothes. I just threw some in, so I hope they're okay."

I took the bag, not really caring about clothes, or what I'd look like. I gazed up at him. "Can I ask you something?"

"More questions?" he said, with a laugh.

"I take it you pay Scott to do work for you?" At his raised eyebrows, I continued hastily. "Sorry, I know it's none of my business, but he's been so kind to me and there's so much work that needs doing to this house. I wondered if maybe you could help him."

"You think I should pay him more?"

His feelings were blocked, which I read as a bad omen.

"No, I mean I don't know what you pay him. I just thought you may feel that helping to keep me safe was a little more important than his usual job."

I held my breath, waiting for his response. His eyes were narrowed in a way that told me he knew I was trying to manipulate him, but then he smiled. "I'll see what I can do about a bonus."

I flung my arms around him again and kissed him.

"Okay, okay," he said laughing, "I guess it will be worth it, judging by that reaction."

I watched through misty eyes as the car drove away. My bare feet cold and sore against the gravel, my heart in my throat.

The next morning, I awoke with my head full of plans for the day. I dressed quickly and took the stairs, two at a time.

"You're awake." Scott smiled and put two plates on the table. "Come and eat breakfast.

He'd made omelettes, and I was starving, so I sat down and tucked in. "Do you know where Tom's cousin lives in Southampton? I thought I might pay him a visit."

"How are you going to get away with that? Tom isn't aware you know Karl. How will you explain how you found him?"

"I won't. He thinks I'm on holiday somewhere and I'll make sure I bump into him. Karl is keeping in touch with him, so I'll know by his feelings if anything happens. Will you take me, please?"

"Haven't you told Karl you're going back to Sanctuary?"

"No, I just promised to stay away from the manor."

"Okay then, but it will take about four hours to get there. We'll leave early tomorrow."

"Thanks, if you stop at a cashpoint I'll give you money for fuel."

"Not a good idea," He said, frowning. "If any hunters are looking for you,, they'd track the card transaction."

"Oh."

"It's fine. You can owe me."

"Thanks. I'll owe you a lot, but I did ask Karl about you getting a bonus."

His eyes widened. "You did what? Are you mad?"

I grinned, "Probably, but he said he would see what he could do. I think that means yes!"

He grinned back, and his face lit up. "Are you absolutely sure you're not a witch?"

The following afternoon, I booked into a bed and breakfast just down the road from where Tom was staying. As luck would have it, the owner, Mrs Martin, laughed as soon as I told her where I usually worked.

"Well, I never! Did you know that lovely gentleman Thomas Ashton is staying just down the road with the Rossiters?"

I pretended I didn't, and told her I'd been travelling around on holiday.

"I bumped into Jean Rossiter in the bakery yesterday, lovely woman she is. She was delighted to have him as a visitor. A bit of restoration going on back there at the Manor I hear. Must be an expensive job maintaining a house like that. Mind you, he has a bob or two. Single as well."

I nodded as she looked me up and down and frowned. I felt a sudden streak of disapproval and assumed she wondered if my intentions were honourable towards the lovely gentleman. "I'm sure he's just waiting for someone with enough class, Mrs Martin. I've seen him with a beautiful girl who rides horses."

This seemed to put her mind at ease about me.

And so, unwittingly, Mrs Martin had given me the perfect excuse to knock on the Rossiters' door and act as if it were pure chance which took me there.

K15

Mrs 'do call me Jean' Rossiter, beamed at me, then ushered me through to the lounge. It was a modern affair, all in white and grey. More showroom than homely. "Tom, you have a visitor dear!"

As he stood, face lit with joy, the depth of his feelings alarmed me. They were almost as powerful as the ones I'd felt from Karl but much less welcome. Had he really been that infatuated with me before and I hadn't noticed, or had his feelings grown during my absence? I felt uncomfortable and wished I hadn't come.

"Jean, this is my good friend Emily." He was so gallant, not calling me his cleaner, I reminded myself that he was a gentleman, whatever his feelings were. Surely, there was no need to worry.

Jean's blue eyes twinkled under her curly grey fringe. "Nice to meet you luv. Would you like to join us for a spot of afternoon tea?"

"Thank you, Jean. That would be lovely." My stomach growled at the thought.

We were ushered through the French doors to a patio area, and Tom and I sat at the garden table.

"I'll pop and get everything ready." She dashed off into the house as a small, rather plump man ambled towards us across the lawn.

"Simon's Jean's husband," Tom explained. He shares my passion for horses. At the mention of horses, Simon's face broke into a wide grin. "Ahh, wonderful beasts." He reached the table and pulled out a chair, plonking his considerable rear onto it. "So, who's this lovely young lady then, Tom? And where've you been hiding her, eh?" He chuckled, whilst Tom's face turned the colour of beetroot.

"Now don't you be teasing him, Simon," Jean chided, appearing with a large tray, laden with cake and tea. "Emily here is a friend of his, and she's very welcome."

"Of course, of course." Simon winked at me and smiled. "Any friend of Tom's, and all that."

I was keen to save Tom from his embarrassment, for my own sake as much as his. The heat of his anxiety was flooding my chest and I could feel it rising up my neck.

"How are the horses?" I asked. Returning to safe territory.

Tom looked at me with gratitude. "Thriving thanks to the great operation Simon and Jean have here."

"We're proud of what we've accomplished here." Simon looked at his wife with unconcealed love. "We own the land from the hill next to Langland farm, right up to North brook cross. It's ten acres in all, with road access and running water. I designed the stables myself. Plenty of room for our own horses and to provide livery for others. Well worth it. You wouldn't believe the amount of money in it, Emily. I keep telling Tom, he should rent out a stable at the Manor."

"I'm not sure about having strangers traipsing about on the land, Simon," Tom answered. "It's different for you; the land isn't attached to the house."

Whilst we talked, I kept glancing at Tom. I was aware his eyes were on me most of the time. Although I told myself he would never act on his feelings, an alarm bell rang in the back of my mind.

"Would you like to come with me and see the horses, Emily? I'm going to the stables to feed them anyway."

I wasn't sure if it was a good idea to be alone at the stables with Tom, but I didn't know how I could say so without offending him, especially in front of his friends.

"That would be nice," I said. Guilt pierced my stomach as his heart pulsed faster.

We took Tom's car and arrived in less than ten minutes. Still, I was surprised Tom didn't want his mares nearer. "Aren't you worried about horse thieves finding them up here?" I asked, as we pulled up in front of the stables.

He shook his head. "Did you notice the farm house we drove past at the bottom of the lane?"

I nodded.

"It belongs to Nigel Greenslade. If anyone comes messing around up here that shouldn't be, he'd be out with a shotgun." He laughed and got out of the car.

I looked in the wing mirror, half expecting a mad farmer waving a gun. Having reassured myself that it was safe I joined Tom. We walked past the stables into the fields, where the two mares grazed alongside the Rossiter's chestnut gelding. I was happy to help carry hay into the field, and watched as Tom made a fuss of Jenna, only to be nudged by Gem who wanted some of the attention.

"They look happy here."

He looked at me and smiled. "Yes, I think they are. What about you, Emily, are you happy?"

Thoughts of Karl flashed through my mind. "Yes, but I miss Kenwood. I guess you do too.

"Not really, but I have missed you." He blushed, looking away quickly.

"Tom, don't." *God, what am I doing? Karl would go nuts if he could hear this.*

"Your friendship, I mean. You're good company."

"Thanks." His lust told me a different story. It crackled in the air between us. Stepping away slightly, I ran my hand over Jenna's glossy coat, changing the subject. "Have you heard anything about the work being done? Is everything okay?"

"As far as I know. Why?"

"I just wondered. I can't wait to get back there. I love that house, always have. I told you before, I feel like I belong there." *But I don't belong with you.*

If I hadn't been an empath, I may never have realised. His face didn't change, but his feelings did. His smile betrayed something dark. It coiled its way into my gut. I froze, my heart turning to lead in my chest. My eyes grew wide with horror. As he stared at me, I finally found my voice. "What is it, Tom?"

He blocked my way out of the stable. Fear and anger twisted inside me. "Tell me what you've done."

"You need to listen to me, Emily. I did it to protect you. Karl should have stayed away from you.

Oh my god, I'm right! "How did you know?"

"I wasn't entirely sure, but he changed. He actually started being nicer to me."

"Isn't that a good thing?"

"Not if he was trying to get to you. Emily, can't you see he was playing games? He was being nice to me to please you. I had a suspicion when you said you were attacked. He was in a foul mood when I returned after Christmas and I wondered if he had anything to do with it, but I couldn't understand why you wouldn't have told me if he'd been pestering you. We are friends, aren't we?"

"I thought we were Tom, but if you've done something to harm Karl, how can I forgive you?"

"You don't understand. You have no idea what he is." His face took on a cruel twist I hadn't seen before.

I rounded on him, "Of course I do. I've always known what he is; he told me himself. And I know about the vampire hunters. You're the one who's put me in danger! I thought Daniel was going to kill me in the car park. I assume you know all about that."

"You were there? My God, I didn't realise. Daniel just said he'd wounded Karl." He reached to touch me, but I flinched away. "Karl's just trying to seduce you in order to wind me up. I didn't think you knew what he really was." He grasped my arms and stepped closer. "Do you know how many women he's killed? How can you blame me for wanting to protect you? I love you, Emily."

His face was too close. I tried to pull away but couldn't. Fear grasped my chest. This wasn't happening. *Was it?* Ana was my enemy, not Tom. I tried to keep him talking so I could think.

"I know he's killed women before, but he does care about me. He really has changed."

"Emily, he's killed every human he's slept with! You had to get away from him. He has to be destroyed."

"Tom, you're wrong. He hasn't killed every woman he's ever slept with. I'm still alive."

His shock hit me like a hammer to my chest and he let me go like I'd contracted the plague. I fell to the ground.

"How could you?" He looked at me in total disgust.

Trembling, I reached into my pocket for my mobile. I wasn't sure if anyone would answer from the house, but I had Scott's number.

"What are you doing, give me that," he growled, wrenching it from my hand. Gone was the sweet man I thought I knew. He threw my phone on the floor, and I gasped in horror as his foot came down on the screen. I heard a crunching sound.

I pulled myself up to a sitting position. "Are you mad? You can stop this Tom, whatever you've done. Have you sent hunters to the manor? They're going to blow it up, aren't they? Have they already planted the explosives?"

He stopped and stared at me, his hazel eyes full of suspicion. "How do you know?"

"I know a lot of things. Like how you were miserable when I first came to Kenwood Manor, but recently you've been happier."

"I thought you cared about me; that's why."

"And I do, we could still be friends if you stop this." His face softened. I took the chance to stand up and place a hand on his arm. His feelings made me feel sick, but I had to calm him down. I needed to get away from him.

For a moment, I felt love run from his arm, to mine. Then his eyes narrowed. "But you will be with him and he will want me dead. Then sooner or later he will kill you."

"I'll talk to him, tell him you were just trying to protect me and it got out of hand. We could blame Daniel."

I felt his uncertainty and thought I could talk him around. I was wrong. He stepped out of the stable quickly, slamming the doors behind him.

"No!" I screamed, throwing my body against the inside of the door. I heard the bolts slide across on the other side.

Tom's voice came through the wood. "No, Emily. This is how it has to be. I'm going now, but first thing in the morning I'll bring food. There's fresh water in the trough, and the hay will keep you warm enough. Tomorrow afternoon it will all be over and I'll let you out."

"You won't get away with it," I shouted. "The farmer will check. He may have seen you bring me here." He was so close to the door I could hear him breathing. I had to keep him there and make him change his mind.

"I've got a bottle of whisky in the car to drop in for him. If he mentions you, I'll tell him you're grooming the horses while we have a drink. Once he's had a few he'll forget all about you." He started to back away. "Goodbye."

"Wait! Why tomorrow if the explosives are already in place?" It dawned on me as I spoke. "Benedikte?"

"Yes. They wanted an original. Mr Stone wouldn't risk his team for Karl. He'd heard there were vampires in the area, but the body count wasn't high enough to risk his men over. Benedikte is a different story.

"How do you know Benedikte will come?" I pressed my hands to the door and tried to peer through the gaps. I could just make out the material of Tom's coat.

"Vampires are proud and arrogant" His voice was harsh and cold. I shivered. They couldn't allow Karl to be harmed without it sending a message that vampires are weak. Tonight Benedikte will arrive at Kenwood. Tomorrow, when the sun is at its highest, Kenwood Manor will be destroyed, and Karl along with it." The coat moved away. His footsteps retreated.

"Come back. Don't do this!" I hammered on the door until I heard the car start up. As the sound of its engine got further away, I sank to the ground and wept.

Alone in the stable, I thought about the films I'd watched where the heroine manages to escape her captor. I tried to shoulder barge the door, then searched the stable for something to unscrew the hinges with. Frustrated and afraid by my lack of success, I kicked and pounded the door until I was bruised and bloody. Exhausted, I decided that perhaps I wasn't heroine material after all. My only hope was to talk to Tom again when he returned with the food.

Time had never moved so slowly. It gradually got dark and colder. I curled up in the hay, attempting to stay warm. I must have fallen asleep for a short while because I dreamt of Sanctuary. Tyler, Lily, and Callum were calling to me, but I was backing away from them, waving and saying goodbye. I stepped backwards and I was falling from the cliff. I could see their faces looking down at me and I clutched the little bag of Angelica root, hoping it would somehow save me. When I woke I thought about the white bag still hanging around my neck. It didn't seem to be working.

I decided, during that long lonely night, that I'd say anything to make Tom change his mind. Eventually, I heard a car and jumped to my feet. Footsteps approached, then Tom's voice called to me.

"Emily, I've brought a sandwich and some bottled juice. Stand back and I'll put it through the door."

I stood still, wondering what to do. He sounded friendly enough.

"Emily. Are you okay?"

Despite promising myself to stay calm, I couldn't hide my fury. "Of course, I'm not bloody okay! I'm locked in a stable." I slammed my palm against the door.

"It's only for a few more hours. I just want to keep you safe. Now stand back and I'll open the top door."

I sighed and stepped back. Perhaps I could still change his mind if I obeyed him. The top door swung open and Tom's face appeared, his brow furrowed. "You needn't worry; I have no intention to hurt you. I've thought about things and I forgive you. It's his fault, he's filled your head with lies, but I know you'll realise it's me you should be with. You just need time."

Forgive me! Was he having a laugh? Did he think I would forgive him? I forced a smile. "You may be right. Do you know where I've been?"

"No. I thought you'd been travelling."

"No. Karl sent me to a place where I'd be safe. I can't really talk about it, but there are people there who I made friends with. I felt happy there, but I missed Kenwood. I thought it was Karl I missed, so I sent a message through a friend for him to meet me. He sent me away, Tom. I know that Ana is with him, he admitted it. I don't trust him, but I'm afraid of him and what he might do to us if you try and harm him."

"He won't be able to. He'll be gone."

I was winning; I could feel it. I took a step toward him. "But what if they fail? If he finds out you had anything to do with it he'll come after you. Why do you think I came here, Tom? I care about you. Ring Daniel and call it off. We could just leave together. Karl will soon forget about us now he has so many vampires there with him."

Tom smiled, but his eyes were sad. A combination of hope and despair tinged the air around him. "I don't know if they'll listen to me now, Emily. They want Benedikte. I'm sorry, but it has to be this way. I know you love that house, but we will rebuild it, I promise. I have millions in the bank and with Karl gone I can use it."

I lunged towards the door, just as he swung the top shut. "Tom, no. Please don't leave me again."

"I'll see you again soon, my love."

He went quiet. Another car was approaching. I shouted, "Help!"

"Emily, if you shout again I'll have to gag you."

I took no notice. To gag me he'd have to open the door. As the engine stopped I shouted again. Tom ran from the stable and I heard muffled voices.

"Help!" I pummelled the door with my fists.

I heard Tom cry out and then footsteps running in my direction.

"Emily?"

It was Scott.

"Here, Scott. Quickly, I have to get to Karl."

The door was flung open, just as the bang of a gun rang through the air. We turned to see a quad bike tearing over the grass. An angry looking man was steering with one hand; waving a shotgun in the air with the other.

Automatically, I raised my hands. Scott did the same. Tom looked to be out cold on the floor. The quad bike came to a stop in front of us, and the man I assumed to be the farmer jumped off.

"What the bloody hell be you doin?" He caught sight of Tom and rushed over, keeping the gun pointed at us.

Scott spoke up. "He had her locked in the stable. Put the gun down. I need to get her out of here."

Tom began to stir. The farmer looked from Tom to Scott. "What this lad here? Why would he lock up that young lass? It don't seem likely to me.

I stood in front of Scott. "It's true. He says he loves me, but I don't feel the same. He reacted badly." We began to edge towards the car. Tom moaned. "Look. He'll be fine, but I have to get away. My friend is just trying to help me. Please." I looked at him beseechingly.

The farmer scratched his head. "Tis true I saw him come up with you. Then he came back to me alone. Said you was grooming. Can't remember after that." The gun lowered an inch.

"He gave you whisky didn't he? Encouraged you to have several, I bet."

Tom began to sit up. As the farmer turned to look at him, we ran.

"Quick, get in the car," Scott yelled, throwing the driver door open and jumping in. I was half in when a shot fired. Tom held the gun now; he was running towards the car. I slammed my door shut and we reversed quickly down the drive. Another blast of shot hit the ground. Then we were on the public lane, racing away at speed.

Through short panting breaths, I said, "take me to Karl."

Scott nodded, keeping his eyes on the road and his foot down.

Once I had my breath back, and the road widened, I turned to Scott. "How come you came back for me?"

"Because I went back to Kenwood and Lord Ashton asked if you got back to Sanctuary safely. He was surprised I'd got you there and gone back so quickly. I told him where you were and…. Well, he wasn't happy. Have you seen his eyes go red? Scares the shit out of me. I wish you'd have a bit of thought for my life once in a while."

I hung my head. "Sorry. I thought I'd be safe with Tom."

"Luckily for you Lord Ashton didn't."

"He knew?"

"No, but he wasn't sure. He knows Tom loves you and if he'd found out about the two of you, he would have a motive."

"I wish he'd shared his suspicions with me. How did you find me?"

"I was following Tom. I went to that guest house first and the lady told me you had gone to visit Tom. He was leaving the house just as I was pulling up outside. I lost sight of him because of the temporary traffic lights, but when I saw there were stables here, I guessed that's where he would be. I wasn't expecting to find you locked up, though."

"I still can't believe it was him, Scott." For a moment, our shared relief clouded my mind, but it came rushing back- the explosives – the danger – Karl! "Shit. We have to warn them, quickly. There are explosives in the house."

Scott fumbled in his pocket with his free hand. He pulled out a mobile. "Why don't you try ringing the house? Someone might answer it."

I dialled the number and waited. It cut to answer phone. I began leaving a message about the explosives and then the phone was picked up at the other end and I heard Karl's voice. *If you're there, God, thank you.*

"Emily, are you okay?"

"Yes, but you have to get out of there. Tom let them plant explosives before you put the new security system in. They've been waiting for Benedikte to arrive. Is he there?"

"Yes, he arrived last night. We were planning to attack tonight."

"Just get out, Karl."

"Don't worry; just go back to Scott's. We'll search the house and I'll call you later."

The line went dead.

From the car window, I looked at the sky and watched the Sun playing hide and seek among the clouds. I'd never been travel sick, but nausea overwhelmed me. I dug my nails into my arms, trying to stop my mind from whirling. A while later the phone went. It was Karl.

"Emily, it's me, we've found the explosives. Prof disabled them."

"Wow! That was quick, where were they?"

"Near the entrance to the tunnel, in the woods, and by the cellar door. They were hidden well, but there are ten of us here now, so it didn't take long to search everywhere."

"What if there are more?"

"We've searched everywhere they could have possibly put them. I still want you to stay at Scott's tonight, but drop in on the way over so I can see you."

After telling Scott the news, we stopped for fuel. I told myself everything would be fine, but my anxiety still danced around in my stomach and rattled my heart.

By the time we got to Kenwood Manor, it was nearly mid-day and the sun had cleared the clouds. Scott pushed the button by the gate, then waited while the big gates swung wide enough for him to enter.

As the gates began to close behind us, another car came racing up the road and swung into the gates, stopping them from shutting properly. Scott stopped to see who it was, and I jumped out just in time to see Tom squeezing out the passenger door, which was partly wedged in the gates.

"Emily wait!" he shouted down the drive. "You can't go in there. It isn't safe."

Scott tried to shove Tom out of the gate, but he was frantically trying to get to me. I decided I may as well face him. What harm could he do now?

I walked towards him. "They've failed, Tom. The explosives have been found. I'm in no danger, but you will be if Karl catches you here."

"What do you mean they've found them? Where?"

I repeated what Karl had told me, aware of the sun's warmth on the back of my neck.

"What about the ones in Karl's quarters?"

"Nice try! Even I know you can't have got in there. Only Karl has that code. He won't even let me see it."

"Well, I guess I outsmarted for once. I guessed the number. Not many numbers could mean anything to Karl. He used Toby's birthday."

His words cut through me. *Oh my God. Lily's vision. Tyler warned me not to come here.*

I still don't remember exactly what happened next. It's like the world went blurred. I must have run towards the house. I remember shouting at Scott to get out, and I remember feeling I had to warn Karl. Tom was shouting my name. *Did he follow me?* I don't know. I saw the front door getting bigger in front of me, and I was shouting Karl's name and "Get Out!" over and over.

Then the world shattered around me.

Was I propelled by the force of the blast, or did I smell his scent and hear my name as I twisted in the air, then fell face down on the grass, something heavy on my back? My feet suddenly burned red hot; a searing pain through my body, but the rest of me was cool.

Was he there?

I wondered at this for a fleeting moment, before my world went black.

K16

April...

I seem to be suspended between land and sky. Perhaps I'm floating.

All is black, but I'm not afraid. The sound of distant voices tease my ears. They're familiar and friendly, but I can't make out what they say. I want to move, but my mind seems distant from my body.

Still I'm not afraid. The smell of a familiar scent lingers in my nose. This makes me feel happy, though I can't remember why. I sense I must wait, though I've no idea what for.

My mind drifts back. I see my old playhouse again... I'm still inside making mud pies... picking peas in the garden and eating more than I save... then pretending to shoot my brother with a toy pistol...sunflower wallpaper in my bedroom...reading books in the attic...

Voices penetrate. I try to cling to my favourite memories. The voices become clearer. My body is jerking and shuddering; I can't control it. I feel pressure below me; my body hurts. I hear words, but I can't understand.

Now I am afraid.

The shuddering eases as blurred faces swim into view. I feel them near me, though I can't see their faces. Love and anxiety stir my insides.

There's a gently shushing noise and a constant beep, there are muffled voices floating around me... and then... a woman's voice...

"Hello, love you're in hospital, but you're going to be fine."

I managed to flick my eyes from side to side, trying to see why my arms jerked up and down.

"It's the anaesthetic wearing off, dear. You've been in an induced coma…..burns…..skin graft."

I recognised Mum's voice and struggled to take the words in. I looked into her glistening, blue eyes. *What? My feet hurt. Did you say skin grafts? Why? What the hell happened?* I felt a gentle hand on my now relaxed arm. My eyes moved to Dad's face. He smiled. *If I'm going to be fine, why is anxiety coming off you in waves?*

I tried to speak, to ask what happened, but there was something in my throat. I squeezed their hands to reassure them, trying to take the worry off their faces. Something bad had happened, something really bad. But what? I looked up at them, waiting to hear more.

Dad stroked my arm. "Relax, Emily." His even voice soothed me. "You're safe now. We're here to look after you."

I listened as Mum told me I'd been in an explosion at Kenwood Manor. An image came back to me. The Manor… at a distance, through the trees, when I was a child. Mum said I'd worked there recently, but I couldn't remember.

Dad said I'd been lucky. The ground around me had been scorched, but only my feet had been burnt. It was as if something had landed on me and covered most of my body, breaking several ribs and the femur in my right leg, but saving my life.

I desperately wanted to remember. I had a fleeting memory of a familiar smell. The face of a person began to form in my mind but faded before I could make out who it was.

The next day, the nurses pulled the tube out from my nose. I gagged the whole time; my eyes filled with tears. They told me it was a feeding tube. They hoped I'd be able to start eating properly.

Later, when I tried to talk, my voice didn't seem like my own. It sounded different and far away.

I asked the nurses questions when mum and dad weren't there. I wanted straight answers. "Why haven't my friends or my brother Gary been in?" I asked a nurse.

"Because you're in an intensive care unit and we have to restrict visitors. I'm sure we could arrange for your brother to come in, if you like?"

I nodded. We'd argued a lot when we were young, but if I was ill, he would tell me stories, even before he could read the words properly. I remembered him buying me a mug with his pocket money too. Suddenly, I needed him.

"Why am I in intensive care?" a sudden thought jolted my heart, "Could I die?"

The nurse placed a hand on my arm. "No. We need to monitor the skin grafts closely to ensure your body accepts them. There aren't enough staff on the main wards to check and dress them every three hours."

"And if they don't work?"

She fixed her eyes on mine and smiled. "You're through the first twenty-four hours. That's a very good sign. I have to tell you there will be scarring, but with care, it should be minimal."

"Why can't I remember?" I heard the quiver in my voice as fear crept up my spine.

"There could be more than one reason. You did have a bump on your head, but scans didn't pick up any major trauma. That doesn't mean you won't suffer from temporary amnesia. The shock alone can do that. You lost a lot of blood when your femur broke and nicked an artery."

"So it's temporary?" I swallowed hard, trying to push my fear back down.

"We can't be sure, but we hope so. It's amazing you weren't hurt more. The policeman who came in with you said he can't figure out how you survived and why your burns weren't worse. You were wearing a charm around your neck; I said maybe it protected you. He thought I was slightly crazy, but one thing is certain: something saved you."

I needed to remember what had happened. Could this charm jog my memory? "Can I see it?"

"We gave it to your parents along with your watch. I'll ask them to bring it in."

The wait was frustrating, even though I slept on and off through most of it. Images danced in my dreams. A tiny grave… a photo of a child… blood dripping slowly from a plastic bag… a book…

I awoke, confused. Every waking moment meant running through the maze of my mind, trying to grab hold of something useful.

When my parents brought the charm in, I held it in my hand and studied it. A dirty piece of cloth tied at the top with a thin piece of leather. I tried to untie the bag, but my hands were weak. Mum untied it for me, to reveal some dried bits of plant. It looked familiar, but that was all. Disappointment swallowed me whole. I was lost.

As my feet began to heal, the pain got worse, until the specialist put me on a cocktail of drugs that made me unsure when I was awake and when I was dreaming. In my lucid state, I understood the pain was a sign of healing.

I dreamt of witches, wolves and vampires, then awoke with a feeling I'd almost remembered something important, but it was just out of reach. I saw faces when I was awake and when I was asleep.

One face, I kept seeing. I recognised him, but his name still eluded me.

Without the tube, I had to feed myself. The nurses helped sometimes, or my parents. But sometimes I had to do it myself. I cried tears of frustration, as I tried to lift the food to my mouth – once, twice, three times – it was so tiring.

How can feeding myself be so hard? Even when the pain was under control, I didn't have the strength in my arms to lift the spoon. The nurses said it could be the drugs, the prolonged exposure to anaesthetic while the surgeons carefully moved skin around my body and fixed my bones, and the lack of real food. *I* wondered if it was the constant barrage of anxiety from frightened families in the intensive care unit. Including my own family.

Gary came in and spoon-fed me. I would have been humiliated if I had enough strength to care. I couldn't manage to eat enough over the next couple of days, so the tube went back down.

The dreams continued…I was moving fast. I could tell by the way my hair whipped around my face and the scenery sped past me. I was on a motorbike, clinging to someone; someone tall.

I was on the moors and a man called my name. He held a book that I knew was important. I tried to reach him, but he kept getting further away. I went to call out Heathcliff, but I knew that was the wrong name. Then it came to me.

Karl!

"Karl" Trying to call his name, I could only croak. I surfaced from the dream, pulling at the feeding tube.

Beeeeeeeeeeeep…

I wondered if I was dead; it would explain why nothing seemed real. Had I flat lined? Then a nurse connected the pulse monitor to my finger again. I must have knocked it off. I continued pulling at the tube and trying to call for Karl. I somehow managed to get his name out. "Karl!"

I was pinned down by nurses. They pulled the tube out properly, telling me I'd need to eat. I nodded weakly.

"Who's Karl, pet?"

This nurse was called Cathy. I liked her. She had calm feelings even when things were hectic.

"I'm not sure, but I think he should be here."

I felt lost when they moved me out of intensive care and onto a main ward. It meant I could have more visitors but I didn't see so much of the nurses

The skin grafts had taken well although I was still on drugs for the pain. Everyone seemed confident I was improving. I continued to try to fill the gaps in my memory. I *had* to find the missing pieces.

As soon as I was moved, Holly came to visit me. I was propped up against pillows, and it was wonderful to see her smiling face.

She chattered on about her work, and then suddenly became serious. "Emily... what do you remember about Karl?"

"Do you know him?" I asked, searching her face for clues.

"I never met him. You had a fling with him, but it's over."

I thought for a moment. "I remember his face. He was gorgeous. Dark hair, green eyes. I think I loved him." I smiled at Holly, but she was frowning.

"Emily, he was dangerous. Do you remember Daniel Stone?"

Daniel Stone. A chill ran through my bones. "Who is he? How do I know him?"

"We met him at a bar."

Fear coursed through me. "Oh, God. Tell me I didn't."

Holly gave a laugh. "No, no. But I did." Her face darkened. "I wish I hadn't." She filled me in with the details she knew. Daniel searching for Karl, me warning her that Daniel was using her. "I'm sure you loved Karl, Emily, but I'm also sure he's dangerous."

I creased my brow, trying to remember something; anything. "I don't understand. When I try to remember Karl, I get warm feelings, safe feelings. But when you mentioned Daniel... Are you sure it isn't Daniel who's dangerous?"

She shrugged. "Perhaps they both are. I told the police what I know, which isn't much."

"Police?"

She placed her hand on mine. "Don't panic. They have to question anyone who may know something about the explosion. Your mum told them I was your best mate. Don't worry. It's not as if you did anything wrong."

I faked a smile. *Did I do anything wrong? I wish I could remember.*

When I did remember, I remembered suddenly. And violently. I use that word because it felt like a physical and mental blow.

I was asleep and dreaming of running, not from something, but towards it. Boom! The world changed around me. I felt searing hot air across my feet as something knocked me to the ground.

It was him! I realised it and my panic rose. I screamed his name and woke as nurses came running.

I tried to convey I was scared that he'd died. Then I remembered what he was. Could he die? I don't know what else I screamed and babbled, but I was sedated.

I woke again. My parents were there, saying something about imagination and drugs and bumps on the head.

"What are you talking about?" I croaked. My mind was foggy and I felt as helpless as a child.

"You were shouting about vampires and vampire hunters, dear," Dad said. "It's the medication you're on."

I shook my head to clear it. "Ask Tom. It's true. You need to check Karl's okay. Ask Tom." I grasped Dad's hand tightly.

He looked at Mum in a way that told me something was wrong. I screamed and tried to get out of bed. The nurse ran over.

She stuck a needle in my arm.

When I came around again, Mum and Dad were looking at me. They glanced at each other.

"I think we can tell her now," said Dad, gravely. "You're right. She needs to know the truth."

Alarm ran through me like a bullet train. Truth! What truth?

Mum squeezed my hand. "Your friend Tom." She squeezed tighter. "He was killed, love."

"Tom!" Sadness wrapped itself around my heart. He'd hurt me, but in the end, he died trying to save me. I wiped a tear from my eye. "I remember Tom. He was good to me."

Mum passed me a tissue. "He was dead by the time an ambulance arrived, love. He wouldn't have suffered for long. There was a man called Scott. He called the emergency services. I think they treated him for shock, but otherwise, he was fine."

I mopped my tears. "Karl. Was he...?"

"No," Dad cut in. "No other bodies were found. Whoever Karl is, he couldn't have been there."

They didn't mention my talk of vampires again.

Later, I had calmed enough to realise my parents couldn't help me. Holly may believe me. But she thought Karl was a danger to me, so I couldn't ask her to help me get information. Someone at sanctuary would help me, or Scott. I asked for a phone and called Scott. He was out, so I left a message.

My strength was coming back.

I settled for the night, but I may as well have tried sleeping in an airport runway. As always, there were lights in the aisle and the noise of trolleys being shunted around. And Karl on my mind. In the near-darkness of the ward, I wept, not knowing if I would ever see him again.

Through the morning, I tried to catch up on my sleep and managed to doze. My eyes snapped open to the sound of my name. I swivelled my eyes toward the voice I'd heard. It sounded familiar.

"Emily. Hi." Scott came striding towards me with a rather tatty, but pretty bunch of flowers.

"Thanks. I'm glad you came." I gave him a weak smile. Worry prevented it from reaching towards my eyes.

"Is Karl, okay? I need to know. What happened to him?"

"Karl who?"

I laughed at first, thinking he was joking. Then I sensed his unease.

He looked around at the other patients, all busy chatting to their own visitors or reading magazines, then back to me. "I'm sorry about your accident. You've had a rough time, but I think it may have… well…messed with your head a bit."

Anger welled up inside me. What was he saying? What was he playing at? "Don't be stupid, Scott. I'm perfectly sane, and we both know damn well who Karl is. Why are you doing this? Please, Scott."

He turned away, avoiding my gaze. But he couldn't avoid my so-called gift. So when he said, "I don't know anyone called Karl," I felt his shame, and it intertwined with my fear and my anger.

In hindsight, I can understand why Scott denied knowing anything about Karl or what may have happened at Kenwood Manor. I know he was protecting the people of Sanctuary and protecting himself from vampires who didn't want anyone acknowledging their existence. I understand that now, but at the time, all I could think about was Karl and needing to know he had survived.

So I lost it.

I lashed out, trying to grab his arm and make him talk to me.

"I have to go, Emily." He pushed me away from him and stepped away from the bed.

He has to talk to me. He has to tell me the truth! The words went around in my head, blocking out everything else but Scott and Karl. Gathering up the little strength I had, I launched myself out of the bed. My arms reached out for him, but I'd forgotten my broken leg. I screamed as I hit the floor, but adrenaline kept me moving forward. I pulled myself along the floor with my arms. Scott's feet had hesitated in their retreat.

"Stop him, please." I croaked, as several other pairs of feet appeared next to his.

"Help her." Scott shrieked, as the arms of some nurses appeared at my sides. "She just went crazy!"

I lashed out at the nurses who tried to help me. *Crazy. How dare he!* I shouted Scott's name, then Karl's, as they carried me to the bed.

"Emily!" I heard Mum call.

The nurses held me down, but I turned my head to see Scott leaving, and my parents' anxious getting closer. Their fear hit me from across the room.

I noticed the glint of a needle in the corner of my eye.

Terror claimed me before the drugs did.

October…

Six months ago today I was transferred to a secure psychiatric unit called Elm Lodge.

Six months of people thinking I'm mad if I tell the truth.

Six months of not knowing where Karl is. If he is.

Six months of worrying about the Manor I loved.

Six months of counselling, which has only ever made me feel worse.

They put me in a room with only a mattress and a nurse for company.

No privacy. No comfort. No rights.

They are killing me with their drugs and their imagined kindness. I draw my pain to the outside by biting or scratching my skin until it bleeds.

I feel their pity and I know they are genuinely trying to help me. But how can they?

There is no one to back up my story or no one who is willing to, so you will have to make up your own mind.

Some days, I wondered if he'd gone forever, but the thought was too painful and I banished it straight away. Some days, I wondered if he had ever existed at all.

I've had too much time to think, too much time to feel. My only distraction; the shuffling of other patients escorted down the corridor outside my room.

I gradually feared the doctors were right, that I had a psychotic episode, that maybe I'd been hallucinating.

My days were filled with fear. Every waking hour was torturous confusion. *If Karl isn't real, what is? Am I? Is anything?*

Sometimes, I was escorted to a common room to meet the other inmates. At first, I thought they were all loopy. Some chanted, some shouted, some looked catatonic. Then I wondered. What if they're all perfectly sane, but they see a different reality to the doctors and nurses. What if none of us should be here?

The drugs kept me calm, but didn't stop me from remembering, and nothing could stop me from feeling. *Surely, you can't hallucinate feelings?* I could still feel his feelings as if they were forever linked with my own.

Then there's the nurse with the sad eyes. Her name is Lucy and I have a feeling she believes me. I don't expect she will ever admit it, but she must think I may be telling the truth because I sense her fear. And when she gives me medicine, I can feel her doubt.

This has given me strength. If she can doubt I've imagined this whole story, if she can believe even a small part of it, then I can have hope it's true and that he is still out there.

I began writing my story, hoping someone would believe me. Lucy gave me the paper and a pencil – I'm not allowed a pen, and the pencil mustn't be sharp.

It feels important to be believed, but if you don't, I understand. Either way, I'll get through this, because I believe in myself.

I know what I saw; I know what I felt. If he is still out there, I hope one day he will read this, and know I never forgot him.

K17

Today…

7.00 am
A nurse handed me my medication. I hid the pills under my tongue, as I've been doing for over a week. I feel stronger and more determined to get out. Smiling, I told her I hadn't had any strange dreams for a couple of days.

She patted my arm. "That's good. You're getting better. Your medication's working."

I'm getting better at saying the right thing.

She left, and I spat the pills out into a tissue.

7.30 am
I was surprised to see a nurse, Sally, again already. I was previously on twenty-minute watch due to self-harming and so-called psychotic episodes, where in my confused and frightened state, I told the truth. But since my renewed belief in myself, I've behaved in a manner which most people consider normal.

The nurse handed me a brown paper bag. I could feel the shape of a book. I looked at her; eyebrows raised.

She fiddled with her rings, and I felt her anxiety. "Someone called Scott brought it in an hour ago. I asked if he wanted to see you, but he rushed off."

I remembered the last time I saw Scott, and it filled me with a mixture of anger and guilt.

I slid the book from the bag and held it to my chest, tears of happiness running down my face.

This is my confirmation. I did not make Karl up.

If he'd given me a diamond ring it would never mean as much as my first edition of Wuthering Heights. I'd always thought of the story as a tragedy, not a love story. Now I realised that our story, Karl's and mine, has become a tragedy too.

I remembered the notes Karl wrote to me and opened the book. Disappointment gripped my insides. Turning the book upside-down, I fanned the pages.

My notes weren't there.

8.00am

I tied up my hair in an effort to show I'd started to care about my appearance. The door opened and a different nurse, my favourite, Lucy, walked in.

"Are you ready for breakfast?" she asked, brightly. Then she glanced at the book on my bedside cabinet.

I sensed anxiety and guilt. *Why*?

"Is something wrong, Lucy, you look worried?" *I'm not about to admit I can feel it.*

"No, of course not." Her eyes only met mine for an instant, then darted away. She picked up my notes and scanned them.

"Have you told the doctors how much better I am? I want them to review my case."

She looked up and smiled, her anxiety subsiding. "Yes, I have, but they don't want to rush things. If you leave too soon you could end up back here again. You don't want that."

She glanced at the book again, and there it was; that guilty feeling.

"It's a gift," I said, holding the book and hoping to draw her out.

Her face turned red, as she replaced my notes. "Yes, I was here when that man came in. I checked it and asked Sally to bring it up."

My heart bounded around in my chest like a Labrador puppy. "Were there any letters?"

I held my breath, fully expecting her to deny it, even if she had seen them. *Please, please say you have them.* For a moment, she looked at me in silence. Fear showed in her eyes and it crept into my chest.

"What are you afraid of?" I asked.

"Nothing!" She gave a nervous laugh, then looked at her feet, shifting slightly.

I heard muffled voices outside my room and Lucy began rearranging my pillows. I crossed to the open door as a patient shuffled passed, head down, flanked by two doctors. Closing the door, I turned back to Lucy.

Her eyes met mine and she sighed. "It was two weeks ago. I left the night shift to go home, and... I felt I was being watched. In the car park. I told myself not to be so silly, but I made a beeline for my car. Then I saw something – a shape, but it moved so fast I couldn't see what it was. I thought it might some kind of animal.

"Anyway, I got in my car, slammed the door and started the engine. I was just going to pull away, and I got the fright of my life." Her eyes widened. "A voice, right behind me!"

My heart soared. "It was him!"

She glared at me. "Yes. Him. Your boyfriend, I imagine. Scaring me to death."

"I'm sorry. You must have been terrified." I sat on the bed and gestured for her to do the same. I sensed her hesitancy. *I bet it's against the rules.* "I guess he didn't think. Look, he's really important to me. Please, tell me more."

I watched her shoulders relaxing, then she perched on the edge of the bed. "Well, he asked how you were. I tried to look around, but he put a hand on my shoulder and told me to look ahead and answer the question. I was scared half to death, I can tell you. I'm surprised I could find my voice at all. I thought, to hell with confidentiality, and I told him you weren't doing very well, that you were hurting yourself."

217

My jaw dropped. "What did he say?"

"He was quiet for a moment, then he told me to give you hope. I asked how I was supposed to do that, and he said I should simply believe you, and that would be enough."

I nodded and smiled; a thousand butterflies fluttered in my chest. *He knew I would pick up on her feelings.*

Lucy reached into her pocket and pulled out a bundle of notes, notes I know so well. She laid them on the bed beside me, then stood and tugged at her apron.

"I only took them so no one else would see them. The doctors think whoever Karl is, he's the reason for your psychosis. They think the explosion triggered it, but that you'd been treated so badly you remembered him as a monster and were too scared to get better."

"Is that what you believe?"

Her blue eyes met mine. "I don't know what to believe, but I got the feeling he loves you."

I leapt up and hugged her. "Thank you. You don't know how much you've helped me."

Returning the hug, she said, "You're welcome, but I'd rather you didn't let on I've given you the letters."

I released her and stepped back. "It's our secret. But I have to get out of this place before I go mad. Can you put in a good word for me? Please."

She nodded and left.

Sitting on the bed, I sifted through the familiar love notes, reading them, touching them. My heart leaped as I spotted a piece of folded paper I didn't recognise. It was in Karl's handwriting and much longer than the rest.

Dear Emily
Forgive me for not writing sooner. I took several months to heal after the explosion and have only recently learnt where you are. You must feel so

*alone, my love, and I'll do anything to be with you
again.*

*Benedikte managed to drag me into the woods
before the emergency services arrived. He's much
faster and stronger than me and thankfully only
suffered mild burns. I remember him telling me
you were alive, then I remember nothing for a
long time, except pain.*

*Benedikte and Ana looked after me. Apparently I
was not a good patient! I hope you don't still
worry about Ana. You must know by now that I
love only you. When I heard you shouting my
name I came to you as fast as I could. If only I had
been faster. If only I had listened to you sooner.
You were the most precious thing in the world to
me then, and you still are. You must get better
Emily; I am nothing without you.*

*I was angry with Scott when I found out he had
allowed you to be taken to that place. He thought
he was protecting me, but I would sooner he'd
protected you. I forgave him when he returned
the portrait of Toby. It was tucked safely away
with your clothes. Thank you for looking after it
for me.*

*I asked Scott to bring the book to you, and my
letters so you'd know I am waiting*

*They've probably told you that Kenwood Manor is
in ruins, but don't worry, Emily, we will rebuild it.
It will be even better than before and you will be
the lady of the Manor.*

*I miss you, Emily, I miss you like the only part of
me that matters is missing.*

Please come back to me,

K

XXXX

Now...

I gaze at my empty plate. I've eaten *all* of my breakfast for the first time in months, and the nurses are smiling. For once, I don't have to force a smile back. Excitement fizzles through my body and my mind is focused.

I will convince the doctors I don't believe in vampires or witches, or anything else their fragile minds are afraid of. I'll leave here soon, with my copy of Wuthering Heights, my new clothes, the draft of the book I'm writing and the talisman that Callum gave me. The talisman, which I believe saved us both.

Our story may be a tragedy, or it may be a love story, but this is not the end. This is the beginning of a new chapter. I don't know where it will take me, but I know I'll be with Karl.

He will find me.